AFTERDEATH

MARIUS ANDREI PINTEA

After Death
Copyright © 2024 by Marius Andrei Pintea.

All rights reserved. No part of this publication may be reproduced, distributed, or transmitted in any form or by any means, including photocopying, recording, or other electronic or mechanical methods, without the written consent of the publisher. The only exceptions are for brief quotations included in critical reviews and other noncommercial uses permitted by copyright law.

MILTON & HUGO L.L.C.
4407 Park Ave., Suite 5
Union City, NJ 07087, USA

Website: *www. miltonandhugo.com*
Hotline: *1- 888-778-0033*
Email: *info@miltonandhugo.com*

Ordering Information:
Quantity sales. Special discounts are granted to corporations, associations, and other organizations. For more information on these discounts, please reach out to the publisher using the contact information provided above.

Library of Congress Control Number:		2024911524
ISBN-13:	979-8-89285-168-8	[Paperback Edition]
	979-8-89285-206-7	[Hardback Edition]
	979-8-89285-167-1	[Digital Edition]

Rev. date: 09/16/2024

Table of Contents

PART 1   THE CONQUEROR 1
PART 2   THE GATEKEEPERS 121
PART 3   THE APOSTATES 149
PART 4   THE HYBRIDS 211
PART 5   THE BEARER 233
PART 6   THE WANDERER 263
PART 7   THE DEVOURER 289
PART 8   THE OVERSEER 299
PART 9   THE MANUFACTURER 315

REFLECTION 334
STANDARD V COLLECTOR'S EDITION 338
ABOUT THE AUTHOR 339

PART 1

THE CONQUEROR

Chapter 1

"Ever since I could remember I've always wanted to help people. I just don't know how."

As Johnathan Francis Ketch has this thought echo through his mind, he gracefully flies around the night sky.

His giant golden wings are helping him fly.

Even though these wings are gold in color, they appear to look very naturally made. In terms of texture and design they look like natural bird wings.

"Having the ability to fly gives you a great perspective on things. Before when the wings first started to grow, I thought it was some sort of physical abnormality. Now I think they were given to me to help people."

While he continues to fly with the clouds passing his legs, he has this laser focus on the ground.

He is looking for a random act of crime to stop. This is not the first time he has done this.

He has done this countless times by this point.

The ritual is always the same: go out at night where not many people can see his face. However, the main reason is because he does not want the credit for the deed.

He just wants to help people.

"Going around town helping people and randomly stopping crimes is a baby step. I feel like it is not enough. There is something more I need to do. I just don't know what it is, that's why I'm still searching for it."

Suddenly he sees a woman running away as if she is being chased.

Johnathan moves closer and sees that near her is a drunken man running after her with a knife.

Immediately he flies straight down to the man.

When he arrives just above him, he grabs his shoulders and throws him against the wall closest to him.

This immediately knocks the drunk man out.

The woman does not realize that she is no longer being chased, therefore she keeps running.

Jonathan flies back up to the night sky. He is not seen or noticed by anyone.

While he is still in the air he looks after the woman until she gets to safety.

He looks down at her with his beautiful golden yellow eyes. As his wings continue to flap.

Once he sees that the woman got inside a house, which he assumes is her home, he goes to his.

When he arrives home he lands at the front door of his house.

The moment he lands and is no longer flying the wings fold on his back.

He once again looks around to make sure no one saw him.

This entire town looks like it is from the very first century. However, the more important thing about the town is that it looks like it has not been looked after at all.

Everything in this town looks old and as if it was used countless times.

That is because the town was not looked over very well; it was just kind of dumped and left to the side.

Originally there was a king of this town. However, he was killed at a younger age by another greedy king.

Ever since then no one else dared to try to step up to take his position.

The reason is because whenever someone tried to become king they would be killed.

They would be killed in a very mischievous and sinister way.

A king named Kamar is the one who killed the original king.

At first he just killed the king and left everyone else alone. However, once his son tried to rise up and become the new king Kamar knew he had to make his statement more clear.

The way he did this was by playing along and actually helping fund the "new king's" coronation day.

Once the ceremony was over and they had a final celebratory dinner with everyone they were all poisoned. Not just the "new king", all of his supporters and everyone else who was not on the side of Kamar.

Ever since then no one else tried to take the crown for themselves.

Which of course resulted in this town having no one else to look after it and everyone just being left to fend for themselves. That being said though everyone did try to do the best with what they had.

Jonathan enters the house.

He sees both of his parents waiting for him.

His parents' names are Ophelia and Duncan. They have been married for many years. He looks more Middle Eastern and she looks more of African descent. Since she was sixteen and he was thirty five. Now she is thirty-two and he is fifty one. Jonathan is their only child.

"He's home now. Let's go to sleep."

Duncan says with a relief in his voice.

Both of his parents do just that while he goes to his room.

He has a couple of candles lit up and now a good look can be seen of him.

Jonathan is a sixteen year old teenager. He is taller than your average teenager. He is already six feet tall and five inches. He looks mixed race. Brown hair, with sunning golden yellow eyes. Hair that is medium length. It goes all the way to the top of his neck. He looks like he is medium built. He looks like he does take care of himself physically but he is not a very muscular guy.

He has no scars or bruises on his body of any kind. He does look very dirty though and someone who is not very good at looking clean. His teeth, hair, everything.

While he is changing into other clothes he looks like he has a big smile on his face. That smile of course is from the fact that he knows that he managed to help someone else tonight.

When he lays down in his bed to sleep he goes on his stomach. He actually can't sleep on his back because of his wings. It is actually very uncomfortable for him to lay on his back. It's the equivalent of someone falling asleep on their arm.

When everyone is asleep in this house it feels very lifeless.

It's a house made entirely of stone and a very basic layout. Barely any kind of decorations in the house. It has no personality or charm to it.

Chapter 2

As Johnathan wakes up in the morning his eyes slowly open. He wakes up with this great feeling of peace in his heart.

He immediately changes into different clothes. However, he puts on multiple pairs of clothes at the same time.

This is to help him cover up the wings on his back. This is uncomfortable for him. He does feel like he has no other choice though. This of course makes him look a lot thicker.

While walking to school he constantly has the urge to just start flying. He only wants to fly to school because it saves him more time.

Of course the thick clothes and walking to school are all about blending in to not give his secret away.

That being said though that does not mean it affects him any less emotionally or mentally.

There are a lot of other kids at this school and even some of the teachers who look at him in a strange way.

The height is the least of his problems.

Nothing happens though he just takes every single comment that is said about him.

He does perform well in school.
The thing that needs to be taken note of is that when he is taught history, or any other subject that is much more related to a lot of memorizing he does fine.

If it is a subject that requires a lot of physical activity he performs very well in it. Although in those subjects that require memorizing if anything in all that studying is related to fighting, battling, or any other kind of situation that requires physical altercation between two or more people he is glued to it.

His brain tattoos that on itself the second he hears it.

Due to his taller frame and physical activity at night outside of school it resulted in him doing a lot better in all the physical sports activities at school. Also, his taller frame makes him look more imposing and threatening even though he has no intention of ever acting like it.

That also makes a lot of the kids in the sports activities in plays feel like they need to put in minimum effort on their part. That is to not upset Johnathan thinking they will attack him back.

While sitting in class and just listening to his teacher giving a lecture a sudden feeling hits Johnathan.

"Enjoy the moment. Very soon you will have so much pressure on you that it will be overwhelming. This feeling of peace must be preserved for as long as possible."

This feeling did not just stay with him during this class it actually stayed with him all day. He couldn't help, but feel excited about it.

At lunch time he sits alone. He does this on purpose to keep an eye on everyone.

Just in case he needs to step in at the last moment and help someone.

Everyone else is sitting next to someone while he is alone. This does not bother him at all.

Jonathan just naturally looks like the kind of person who likes being alone.

The main thing he is doing right now is just scanning the room looking for someone to help.

Someone to save.

No one needs to be saved.

He looks out the window at the bright yellow sun, "the sun needs to set soon. The night sky must arise. There must be someone out there who needs help. I'm useless in the daytime."

While he continues to eat he hears the conversations of other students.

He is not eavesdropping on them, he just so happens to hear what they are saying.

"Did you hear about THE WINGED MAN making another appearance last night?" Says one student.

"You mean THE GOLDEN PHOENIX? Yes I heard." Says another student.

"This must be like the one hundredth appearance of him in a row? I'm sure there is more. He must be a guardian angel or something. Sent from the gods and born by gods to protect us." A third student just jumps into the conversation.

"I wonder why he is literally made of gold. That must be some very heavy and difficult armor to put on." A random student just speaks out loud.

Jonathan is trying to hold his excitement while hearing all of this. It is very clear to him what he is doing. People are not only noticing, but it is working.

When the second school ended he rushed home as quickly as possible. He runs home so quickly that the way his wings bounce up and down they almost slept out of his clothes.

He runs right up the stairs to his room and looks right out the window at the sun.

Waiting for it to finally set again.

While waiting, he takes off all of the shirts he has on. This results in his wings being able to stretch, just like any other muscle.

Jonathan once again is among the stars. Plus the night sky is fresh and the moon is bright and full.

He looked everywhere for someone to save.

Surprisingly, there is no one. The whole town is very quiet. This confuses him. It actually makes him very uncomfortable how quiet the town is.

Finally while looking around for what felt like forever, he sees a brocade of horses with soldiers on them. While other soldiers are on foot.

In front of this brocade there is a small child. He is only ten years old. However, he has a crown on his head.

This is Kamar Gangi. He is covered in purple from head to toe.

He has brown hair and eyes as well. He is also mixed race.

All the soldiers are covered in armor. Same with the horses.

Kamar looks around and realizes that everyone is in their homes.

Suddenly the soldier next to the king pulls out a trumpet. He plays on it a little bit clearly trying to get attention. As if some sort of announcement is about to be made.

The noise does end up waking a lot of people. They cautiously look out their windows and doors.

Jonathan can sense that something is wrong. Therefore, he flies closer. Not close enough to be seen though.

"This town is quiet. They should be celebrating that their king has arrived. Maybe if I light the first spark then the celebration can begin."

Another soldier grabs a torch and looks for the closest house to throw it at.

Jonathan realizes what is about to happen so he flies straight down.

He knows he is about to be in a very dangerous fight. He has never fought before and he knows that he could die.

As soon as this thought enters his mind then this armor starts to form a perfect outline of his body. It comes from underneath his skin and starts to mold itself onto him. This does hurt him as it comes out of his skin. However, it has happened so many times that to him, it's like ripping off a band aid.

The armor is also gold and the armor outlines his body so perfectly that he looks like a statute. The mask has check bone outlines on it, his stomach guard looks like it has perfect abs on it. His arms and legs look perfectly protected. Even the wings turn metallic.

When he lands on the ground he looks like a soldier ready for battle.

This armor also increases his height to six feet and eight inches.

Chapter 3

The soldier who is about to throw the torch is stopped in his tracks by fear.

He throws the torch out of fear at Johnathan.

Every single soldier and horse on Kamar's side freaks out.

"Leave now no one wants you here!"

Jonathan's voice sounds different. However, it's just quieter because of the mask. There is still a line on the mask across the mouth for him to be heard out of.

Everyone is taken aback by what they have seen because to them it just looks like a god came out of the clouds and just landed here.

Jonathan speaks again, "Please. Your majesty, I don't want trouble, just leave."

All the soldiers have their arrows drawn right at Johnathan.

Even though Johnathan does have a mask over his face he clearly looks nervous.

"STOP!"

Kamar's shout was so authoritative that all the soldiers lowered their weapons.

"Who are you?" Kamar continues to speak.

Jonathan replies in a very stern tone, "Concerned citizen."

"You don't know your king?"

"I know who you are. I've never seen you here before."

"It's your lucky day. You get to officially meet me. However, since I am your king you must answer all of my questions. Also, answer them honestly. Again, I ask you, who are you?"

"I already answered your question. Your highness…"

"I don't believe it was an honest response."

"I'm just trying to help people."

"Who sent you?"

"No one. I only want to protect people in any way I can. That's the only reason I'm here."

"YOU think that you need to protect these people from me?"

"Well, you were just going to light that house on fire."

"Who are you to tell me this? I am the king. I am ruler of countless towns, villages, and cities. I even have a couple of kingdoms entirely under my control. You can't stop me from doing what I want."

"I just did."

The king now clearly looks angry.

"It is my birthday. Especially on this day I can do as I wish."

"That does not mean I can't stand in the way."

Kamar has this look on his face as if he wants to kill him.

He does not act on that thought. He just sits there for a moment and thinks.

"You have my word that I won't harm anyone. On two conditions: the first is that you come with us.

With those wings that you have there is clearly something very special about you."

Jonathan thinks for a moment about that, before even the second condition can be stated. He has this instinctive feeling to not trust the king. That being said he does know that if he says not to this condition he knows the situation will get worse.

Therefore, he nods to the king.

"The second condition: you have to fly me back home."

"Excuse me?"

"I've always wanted to feel like I was flying in the sky, in the stars, like birds. I deserve to experience it at least once."

Jonathan nods again.

The king gets off his horse and walks to Johnathan.

He is right in front of him. He reaches his arms up as if he is waiting to be picked up.

Jonathan picks him up and he starts to fly. Slowly and steadily flies towards the king's home.

Jonathan is holding Kamar like a baby. That results in Kamar cradling himself in Johnathan's arms as if he is cuddling Johnathan.

Jonathan's eyes are speaking volumes right now. He has no idea what is happening and is just in disbelief right now. He feels very awkward right now.

Kamar asks, "How did you get these abilities?"

"I was just born like this?"

"Was your mother a witch? Were your father's sexual preferences birds?"

"Excuse me?"

Kamar looks at him like, you heard what I said.

Jonathan changes the subject, "I suppose I should thank you. This is the first time I ever left my home."

The king responds with a condescending smile, "You are very welcome. I am a very generous king."

"Show me your face."

"I don't know how."

"Are you trying to jerk me around? You don't want to see me get very upset."

"I mean, I honestly don't know how to show you my face. When I'm 'in attack mode' it's like this armor just turns itself on."

"What does it take to make the armor turn off?"

"My guess is as good as yours. Usually it is when I'm not fighting someone, or feel like I'm being threatened."

"Have you tried giving your power to anyone?"

"I don't want to give my power to anyone. Even if I did, I wouldn't know how."

"I'm guessing you've tried to give your powers to others before?"

"Of course."

Kamar looks a little agitated. However, he tries to mask it by looking around and trying to look amazed.

"Go higher!"

The king demands as he is trying to reach up towards the moon.

Jonathan does listen to him, however obviously Kamar can't reach the moon. He reaches higher and higher, to the point in fact where Jonathan is concerned about dropping him.

"Be careful your highness!"

The king's face starts to turn red as if he is about to explode.

He has a sudden temper tantrum.

"God damn moon. I will blow you up the first chance I get. I am king therefore, I get whatever I want."

"What if the giver can't deliver what you want? Even if they wanted to give that thing to you."

"There is always a way."

They continue to fly for a couple of hours. The entire time they are flying above the clouds not being able to see anything.

Finally by the time the sun starts to rise again they are at the front gates of the king's kingdom.

Jonathan lands with the king still in his arms.

This landing is much softer than the way he usually lands.

The king hops off of his arms.

"Welcome to Sodom."

Suddenly a bunch of soldiers in the towers take aim and point the arrows right at Johnathan.

Chapter 4

"Lower your arrows, you twats! This man brought you your king home…"

All the soldiers lower their arrows.

Kamar continues, "Please enter. Make yourself at home."

The metal gate opens and the two of them walk inside.

The gate is entirely made out of gold. Also, the door behind it has a purple color to it with a goldish flare on top of that.

The door has the symbol of a snake. It is a golden snake with purple eyes.

The doors swing open.

Kamar walks into the kingdom with open arms and a very calm demeanor to him.

While Johnathan walks around very cautiously. This results in the armor that he has on, stay on.

Jonathan still has this gut feeling that there is still this sense of danger around him.

Kamar takes notice that the armor is still on, but this irritates him.

Everyone else in the kingdom takes more notice of Johnathan than Kamar.

Every single person who lays eyes on Johnathan is amazed. As a matter of fact some are so amazed by what he looks like that they fall to their knees.

Kamar looks around as if he takes note how everyone reacts to him.

"This man is not to be harmed and he will not harm me. Keep away from him!"

This being the first time Johnathan went to any other location outside of his home town he is amazed by everything he sees.

This kingdom looks ginormous. With big buildings and castles. Huts, tents, and homes that are very different in sizes. Every single place in this kingdom looks different. To the point where every single designed location has a different size and shape to it.

There are a bunch of flags with the snake symbol on it. Also, the dominant colors in this city are purple and gold.

Everything looks very elaborately built. However, everything is built in a way it is all meant to please one person.

There are also a lot of people in this kingdom too. As a matter of fact it feels like this kingdom is overpopulated. People of all different shapes, sizes, ages, and genders are here.

Due to the overpopulation there is clearly a lot of poverty. The poverty looks like it was deliberately created.

The main reason being is that certain things in this kingdom are looked after. While others things in this kingdom look like they are completely ignored.

The people being the biggest example of this. The younger population no matter which gender they are look like they are better taken care of.

The younger population have the nicest houses, clothes, and the resources needed to survive to live their best life.

The younger women clearly have physical signs assigned to them to see what is being valued of them.

The older population feel a lot more like slaves to the younger population. On top of that they feel completely ignored.

The older women are covered up all over and do nothing but chores and take care of what is needed. However, the women are not as old as some of the elderly men. Some are no older than forty years of age. While others are clearly a lot higher in age. Such as the sixties and even higher.

The younger women and by "younger" all of them are under thirty are symbolically wearing clothes that shows what the king values in them. All their clothes put enfaces on their chests and lower bodies.

Johnathan is being very observant of everything. Clearly this entire kingdom makes him feel very uncomfortable. So uncomfortable in fact that it puts him in a shocked state. This results in him feeling light headed and even losing strength in his legs. He stumbles a bit because of this.

"Let me get you my physicians, you don't look so good."

Kamar says this in such a reassuring tone that it calms him down.

They both head to the king's chambers.

When they arrive there it looks very gothic.

There are some guards in this castle, but it is mostly filled with random citizens. All of them are women.

Inside, everyone was drinking like crazy. Like there is no care in the world.

The constant drinking results in them being very aggressive towards each other.

The biggest problem that Johnathan has with what he is seeing is that all the women are clearly being used.

They are all half naked from the stomach up and just waiting to be available for the services of the king.

This looks more like a brothel than anything else.

Tears can slowly be seen falling from his eyes. He is so hurt by what is happening that he falls on his behind in shock.

This sadness no longer makes him feel threatened therefore, all the armor goes away.

It retracts completely back into his skin. His clothes look completely scratched and torn apart from the armor going through them.

The king himself finally has this look of amazement.

He gestures to the women to move towards him.

All the women move closer to him. However, very cautiously.

One woman who is the closest one to him puts her hand on his arm.

The other women start to surround him more and more.

Another woman kisses the top of his head.

The other women start kissing him and touching him as well.

Since he has never experienced this before he just lets everything happen.

While this is happening the king pulls out a small knife and holds it behind his back.

He has this look in his eye as if he has a completely clear motivation to what he is going to do with that knife.

He is now on top of Jonathan with a knife over his head. He is holding it with two hands, and in a position as if he is going to attack Johnathan with it.

"If you were born this way, then maybe if I cut out your heart and eat it you'll be able to pass your powers on to me."

Kamar says with a determined tone in his voice.

Jonathan obviously heard that.

The armor turns on suddenly. It covers his body so quickly that two fingers of one of the women gets cut off.

While she is screaming in pain the wings that Johnathan has swing out to the side as if they are stretching.

They hit the ground to shoot Johnathan up into the sky and he flies away.

Kamar screams, "SHOOT HIM DOWN!"

Johnathan has never flown faster in his life.

He is going home.

The entire time he is flying home he is trying to think five steps ahead. He knows the king is going to come back. When that happens he knows he won't be able to keep everyone safe.

This time while flying back he actually stays below the clouds.

He sees a bunch of other cities as well. Even though he wants to admire seeing something new he can't. The reason he can't is because he sees so many bad things happening.

Crimes. Poverty. Inequality, and countless other problems.

This makes him feel so overwhelmed that he does not realize that there is smoke coming into his town.

He flies there as fast as he can to the point where his vision gets a little blurry.

He landed right in the center of a street so hard that it actually made a dent in the ground.

This loud noise of him landing gets the attention of everyone.

All of sudden it looks like this presence just over took his mind.

Chapter 5

This presence gave him this ultimate sense of purpose.

To save everyone.

First starting with this town.

All of Kamar's soldiers are destroying the town and tearing it apart.

Burning buildings to the ground, killing people, raping them, doing everything they can to wipe it out.

The first soldier he sees he flies right towards him and attacks him.

Of course Jonathan has no idea how to use a sword he just uses his fists.

When he hits people, he hits to hurt. He fights in a kind of clumsy way.

He has a basic understanding of how to fight, however he does not know any actual fighting skills.

A lot of the strikes that he delivers to the soldiers are very basic punches and kicks.

That being said though he still does do quite a lot of damage to the soldiers he does attack. The armor that he has on adds more damage.

A lot of the soldiers that attack him back make some good hits. They don't do any damage, though. That's because the armor is stronger than any sword.

If by some luck when he pouches a soldier he is not knocked out, in some way it clearly hurts the other soldiers.

Johnathan does end up killing a couple of soldiers even if he does not mean to.

A lot of them end up running away. The majority of them are actually too scared to fight Johnathan back.

Unfortunately, no one in this kingdom fought alongside him. Every single member of this kingdom either ran to safety or was killed.

Johnathan flies right over to his home.

Everyone left in this kingdom takes notice of this.

He arrives home to see his parents killed.

His father is stabbed to death and his mother was raped and killed.

Johnathan falls to his knees.

Johnathan is clearly very upset and can be heard crying even though he has a mask on.

All the people who followed him back here are right behind him looking at him.

Suddenly they throw rocks at him.

As if it was some sort of instinctual response the wings suddenly hold themselves up as if they are blocking the rocks.

For a solid thirty seconds everyone keeps throwing rocks at him.

When they stop he stands up and turns around.

"I'm sorry I brought so much hurt and sorrow to everyone. I don't know if you'll ever forgive me. Whether you do or not I promise I will do this up to all of you. Even if I have to do it alone I will."

Everyone looks at him completely defeated and not knowing what to do.

His armor goes away.

The first thing he does is go outside and dig two graves.

Then he takes his father, then his mother out and buries them.

He then flies around and looks for anyone that needs help.

Some deny his help. Although the majority of them accept it. Even if they don't want to, they feel like they have to accept the help.

This goes on for quite a long time to the point where some of the people he has helped join him. They join home to be more productive.

All the while all the others who were killed who are members of this kingdom are buried too.

Once that is over and done with, Johnathan goes to the dead soldiers and takes all of their weapons.

The exact same thing is done with all the armor.

He places them all in a storage room.

While he is placing all the weapons in the storage room he sees that some of the people are taking the dead soldiers and mutilating the corpses.

The majority of the people actually shifted their anger from Johnathan to the dead soldiers.

Johnathan takes notice of what is happening so he steps in.

"Stop it. Stop it! ENOUGH! You have every right to be angry! Kamar's people do deserve to be punished, but not this way! We are not going to achieve anything like this! Be we act we have to send them a message that we are standing up to them and we no longer tolerate their power over us. The soldiers that ran away will for sure go back to Kamar. Therefore, he will retaliate and when he does we need to be ready. I know I said before that I can rebuild alone... and I can. BUT! I know if you help me we will rebuild together faster and better than Eden ever was before."

While is talking some of the people get inspired and join him.

After he is done talking the first thing they do is take all the dead soldiers and burn them.

They place them all into one large pile and light a fire.

The fire is so big due to the bodies it's as if the kingdom itself has one light source that everyone can just look at.

Some people go to where all the weapons and armor are and completely repaint them.

They will no longer have this color of purple and yellow.

From now on they will have this color of green. Many different shades of green. When there are some stripes of red in there. More specifically bright red that stands out, like cherry red.

Nonstop overnight they continue to work.

Putting out fires.

Rebuilding houses.

Mending injured animals and countless other things.

Even once the sun rose up they continued to work. No one got any sleep.

While rebuilding the town physically they also focus on rebuilding the kingdom spiritually too.

Everyone in the town is taking note of how true to his word Johnathan was; this helps the kingdom spiritually as well.

The biggest thing that Johnathan realized that this kingdom needs to do is to protect itself. Every citizen in this town needs to learn to fight. It does not matter what gender or age they are.

The majority of the teachers are former soldiers or current ones.

Even Johnathan takes part in this as well, because he knows he can fight, but in a very sloppy way.

Meanwhile, the soldiers that ran away from Eden finally arrive back at Sodom.

When they arrive they can see that Kamar is building his army up to go and fight Johnathan.

One soldier shouts, "My lord! The winged man overpowered us. He killed most of our soldiers and forced us to retreat back here."

The soldier is so out of breath and tired that he falls right to his knees.

Kamar walks right up to him.

The soldier bows his head even lower because even on his knees he is taller than the king.

In a very clearly irritated voice the king asks, "A small army by himself? How?"

"His bare hands."

The soldier responds with such fear in his voice. The words that he just uttered sounded very trembling.

With even more irritation now, "tell me you're fucking joking."

The soldier responds again. This time with a slightly less scared tone.

"I wish I was. That armor that he wears protects him so well, but also gives him great strength. He punched one soldier so hard that he went flying back a couple of feet..."

Before the soldier can even continue to speak, Kamar grabs a knife and stabs him in the ear.

Over and over the soldier continues to be stabbed.

After the ear the eye.

Then the neck.

Then the shoulder and pretty much everywhere else on the body.

While the king is stabbing the soldier and he is crying in pain. The king desperately asks, "Why do I not have the power he has? I was born into this position of. Therefore, why does a commoner have these abilities and not me?"

Even though now that soldier is clearly dead Kamar continues to stab him.

The stabbing noises are so loud that even people around them can hear them.

Everyone is clearly shaken by what they just saw.

"If this man can just take out a small army by himself, then I can't just go back and attack. I need to find an alternate strategy to capture him. A way he won't even see coming."

The soldiers slowly all go to the armory and put all their stuff away.

While Kamar is thinking of alternate ways to deal with Johnathan he enjoys the pleasures of his kingdom.

Women, alcohol, and everything else that can give him any kind of pleasure that can possibly bring him out of the stress of the situation.

After a day of heavy drinking he falls asleep right on top of a pile of women. He sleeps on top of them and the next morning he wakes up on top of them.

Even though clearly he has a very bad hangover and can barely move because he has such a bad headache and dizziness, he looks around him and he realizes what he must do.

He snaps his fingers. Therefore, one of the servants runs over to him.

"Get the carriage ready. I want to go to pay a visit to Charlotte."

The servant answers enthusiastically, "very good my lord.

The king gets dressed and ready to go and is on his way to Charlotte.

The journey is a two week carriage ride from Kamar to Charlotte.

Charlotte is the queen of Solstice. This is kind of her kingdom.

Originally it was her kingdom. Until Kamar attacked.

Charlotte's father originally had three children with his wife. Two boys and one girl.

Their kingdom was actually very peaceful and well looked after for a longtime.

The downfall started when the king died in a hunting accident.

The original king's passion was hunting so whenever he had some down time. He was so passionate about it that he would make challenges for him to make it more fun.

He one day decided to go hunting for a grizzly bear. That was the animal he always wanted to have the head of in his trophy room. He goes to the forest with three other soldiers.

They find a grizzly bear fairly quickly in the forest. He also kills it quickly, by shooting it with a few arrows and stab to the side with his sword.

The king thought it was the mama bear. However, it was just one of the teenage cubs of the mama.

While he was cutting the head off of the teenage bear. The mama bear attacks him out of nowhere.

The soldiers of course come to protect him and kill the mother, but they all get injured badly in the process. By being bitten, clawed at and thrown around by the bear.

The mama bear is killed, but everyone is so badly hurt they don't even make the effort to take it back. Or even the teenage bear head back.

When they get home they try to save the king. They do, but only for a while.

The problem is that even after they treated some of the king's words and was able to somewhat recover he developed an infection.

The infection he got from a bite mark from the mama bear ends up killing him.

The second after he is killed the oldest brother gets crowned king.

His coronation day is literally on the exact same day his dad is buried.

The kingdom slowly starts to go chaotic. The reason is because the oldest brother does not know how to run a kingdom.

That's because he was never taught how to. At the age of fifteen he became king. At that time his brother was twelve and Charlotte was nine.

At the same time Kamar is expanding his kingdom.

When he comes to Solstice he comes here with a sword that is lusting for blood.

He comes in swinging and does not even try to discuss terms or any kind of negotiation with the current king.

He lets his men kill as many people as possible as he goes towards the king.

At this time he was also only six years old.

When he arrived at the king his original plan was to kill him then and there. However, when he saw him face to face, not only did he look like he was ready to fight, but his two other siblings were ready to fight too.

When he lays his eyes on Charlotte he thought she was the most beautiful girl he has ever seen.

She has a darker skin tone and more Latina like features. Only nine years old. With long black hair and glowing brown eyes.

The middle child does not like this, but the oldest immediately agrees.

This instantly created this sense of disgust towards both her brothers.

Kamar does not harm her at all; he just takes her hand and kisses it.

Kamar looks over to the soldiers.

"STOP! Spare the citizens."

He looks over the two brothers.

"Kill those bastards."

Charlotte fights and tries to go to her brothers, but Kamar tries to hold her.

"I agreed to let the citizens live. I never said I'd let your brothers live."

After these words float out of his mouth she no longer fights, because

"If you give me your sister I will spare all citizens in the kingdom."

The middle child does not like this, but the oldest immediately agrees.

This instantly created this sense of disgust towards both her brothers.

Kamar does not harm her at all; he just takes her hand and kisses it.

Kamar looks over to the soldiers.

"STOP! Spare the citizens."

He looks over the two brothers.

"Kill those bastards."

Charlotte fights and tries to go to her brothers, but Kamar tries to hold her.

"I agreed to let the citizens live. I never said I'd let your brothers live."

After these words float out of his mouth she no longer fights, because she knows that he just told the truth.

After both of the brothers are killed the crown is given to Charlotte.

"I need someone to look after this place whenever I'm not here."

This is exactly what happens over the next few years.

Charlotte is in charge, but under the thumb of Kamar.

Whenever Charlotte made a decision that affected "her" kingdom in any way Kamar would have to say yes or no to that decision first.

The one time she did not talk to him about a decision there were brutal consequences.

This decision was something she knew Kamar would not like anyway, but this was her first rebellious thing she has ever done.

She falls in love with a local boy from the kingdom named Antonio.

Their relationship goes on for a good six months. It feels like something out of a fairy tale. The main reason is because it was both of their first relationships.

A spy for Kamar in Solstice tells him about the relationship.

Kamar is furious therefore, he comes here as quickly as possible.

When he arrives he instantly goes to Antonio and Charlotte. They take him to a nearby graveyard.

While Antonio's grave is being dug, Charlotte is being held back by Kamar's soldiers and everyone is forced to watch this.

Antonio and Charlotte look at each other while Antonio is on his knees crying.

Kamar shouts, "I told you the queen is mine. If anyone thinks it's a good idea to share her, this will be the punishment for it."

A soldier is standing right in behind Antonio with his sword as if he is about to strike.

Antiono says to Charlotte, "I love you."

Just a split second later he gets his head cut off.

Charlotte is in tears and sobbing even more now because not only did she just lose him, but at the same time that was the first time Antiono ever said those words to her.

That was all four years ago.
Now just as Kamar is in front of the gates entering the kingdom Charlotte greets him pleasantly.

She is all dressed up for him. The main colors of this kingdom are blue and red.

She is clearly older here. She looks like she has just turned thirteen. And her hair a lot shorter.

She tries to hide the look of disgust that she feels towards him by letting this feeling of shame take over.

The shame comes from the fact that even though she is the queen she is not in charge. Therefore, she feels that a lot of the people in her kingdom have lost respect for her.

Hours have gone by of the two of them just talking. The sun has now officially started to set.

Of course after Kamar tells Charlotte about Johnathan she doesn't believe him.

She actually looks very insulted by what she just heard him say.

"I'll look into it and report back to you." Charlotte states in a careless tone.

As soon as Kamar is gone she sends for one of her messengers to go to Eden to see if Jonathan is real.

All the while, back at Johnathan's kingdom of Eden everyone is still working together.

This time though there is much more of a sense of unity. Everyone listens and helps one another and everyone especially listens to Johnathan now.

The kingdom is not entirely fixed yet. However, there has been so much progress made since everyone worked together that everyone feels like they can start to go back to relax again. There is not really much fear among the people here.

Everyone seems to feel protected and safe due to Johnathan being here.

They seem happier than they ever did before. Even though this kingdom has not chosen its leader officially. Everyone just came to an understanding that it is Johnathan. Due to how much he has helped everyone.

Even when they didn't even know it.

For the first time in decades the kingdom has this overwhelming sense of peace and prosperity towards all of its people.

The main reason is because for the first time in a long time people have a leader that is helping them. Not against them.

"There is somebody coming!"

A random archer shouts from a tall tower.

Jonathan immediately stops everything he is doing and shoots straight up and flies with great speed towards that person.

He lands in front of the person so suddenly that the wind that was gathered because of that great speed knocks the person down.

Jonathan immediately draws his sword.

The person is in such shock that he does not even realize what has happened to him.

"What do you want?"

Jonathan's question was shouted so loudly that it made the man snap out of the shock.

"Please don't hurt me. I'm just a messenger."

The messenger stands up.

Jonathan is an attacking stance.

"Speak!"

"The stories of The Birdman are true."

The messenger said this in such a timid tone.

"Queen Charlotte of Solstice wants to speak with you."

Chapter 6

Charlotte and Johnathan are sitting in a room with a table between the two of them. They are in the council room.

All the other politicians are locked out of the room. As a matter of fact everyone in this kingdom is locked out of the room.

Guards are in front of the door to stop anyone from coming in or even trying to get in.

One of the politicians runs away and writes a letter and gives it to a messenger.

"Can I be brutally honest with you? I feel conflicted about the situation. Helping a Godman help bring worldwide peace does sound appealing. At the same time I don't want to bring my people more harm by helping you."

Charlotte says this to Johnathan in an emotional tone to him.

Johnathan thinks to himself for a moment before speaking, "There will be a lot of people that will die. If you want peace you have to prepare for war and unfortunately not everyone is going to live to see peace afterwards. I promise you this though, once peace is achieved and all evil doers are gone, you will never have to worry about crimes being committed ever again. Also, Kamar will never bother you again. I just can't do it all by myself."

"Why me?"

"From what I've heard you are the one who hates the king more than any other monarch. I need someone like that by my side."

Charlotte responds in a defensive way, "What makes you say that?"

Jonathan starts to sound a little authoritative towards her, "I have eyes everywhere. That's one of the benefits of having loyal friends. They keep me updated on everything. They went all over the world looking for people to recruit. All the while doing some reconnaissance at the same time. You seemed like you were the only one who would want to achieve the same goals that we have and actually feel supported along the way. I know for a fact that if this offer was given to any other queen and king they would help me. Then betray me whenever the opportunity presents itself."

"What makes you think I won't?" Charlotte asks in a sarcastic way.

Jonathan gives a very stoic response, "because you would have done it by now."

Charlotte thinks about it for a moment. She is clearly starting to get a little anxious.

"I don't want to be a conqueror, though."

"I know. You just want what is best for your people. That is exactly why I need your help. I just need you to provide resources for us."

"If I help you, am I in charge of my kingdom when this is over?" This question has such a harsh tone to it. It sounds really like an ultimatum.

"You have my word. I will also provide you with whatever needs you require to help your kingdom prosper."

They shake on it.

Jonathan gets up and walks towards a big window. He opens it and flies away.

As she watches him fly away she is in deep thought about the conversation they just had.

She finally unlocks the door from the inside. The other politicians come inside.

Everyone looks concerned and confused for her.

Charlotte states, "don't worry everything is alright. I just wanted to meet him by myself. Nothing happened, he did not attack me or anything of the sort."

Over the next few weeks Charlotte is coming up with a plan on how to help Johnathan.

One day when she is in this council room with all the politicians then someone knocks on the door.

The knock instantly puts a bad feeling in her gut so she reaches for a dagger.

The knock on the door is heard again.

"Want me to answer it, your majesty?" The politician that asks this question is the same one that ran away and wrote a letter.

The other politicians shield her by creating a shield around her.

The moment that politician answers the door he is stabbed through the heart with a sword.

The guards who were there to protect the door are dead on the floor.

A big guard walks into the room. A voice can be heard behind him, "there is no need to be afraid, Charlotte. It's just me."

It's Kamar.

Kamar continues to say, "I'm not here to hurt you anyway..."

Charlotte responds with a trembling voice, "What can I do for you my lord?"

"You don't seem to understand the terms we agreed upon do you. Did I not make it clear enough how urgent this matter is?"

"Believe me, I understand."

"No! No, you don't. If you really understood the gravity of the situation you would not have let him come here and sit down and talk to you. ABOUT HOW TO DEFEAT ME!"

Charlotte closes her eyes as if she is accepting her fate as if she is about to die.

"Don't worry I'm not going to kill you. I need you. You'll make a fine breeder one day. That being said though, punishment is still something you have to face. Killing one citizen daily was clearly not sufficient enough. Here is what I'm going to do instead of me killing someone randomly in your kingdom daily, ten will be killed. DAILY! Here's the best part: you get to pick who dies."

Charlotte is in complete shock and even shakes a bit.

"I've made it a little easier for you. I already killed one."

Kamar says that while snickering.

"By the way, pick your allies more carefully. He was the one who told me you were talking to Johnathan in the first place."

After a good hour goes by finally fourteen people are picked to be killed.

Kamar stands over all fourteen of these people with Charlotte by his side.

"You are all worshiping demonic figures. The fact that none of you stood up to your queen for conversing with Johnathan you will now be punished. If you want to blame someone for this, blame her!"

The queen is just in tears and her face is cherry red.

"What do you think is a fitting punishment for demon worshipers? Cut their head off? Arrow through the art?"

Charlotte is clearly getting the sense that Kamar is not only taunting her, but all these questions are rhetorical.

"Oh, that's right! We burn them!"

As all of these people are set on fire, the rest of the kingdom is forced to watch.

The screams of agony echo throughout the land.

Charlotte looks at Kamar so intensely while crying that it looks like she is about to snap and kill him.

She almost lets the words, "Keep smiling with that shit eating grin. Very soon you will go to a deep dark place and it will give more relief than anything else has given me before, or I will ever feel since then."

However, those words don't slip out of her mouth and just keep them in her head.

Now back at Kamar's castle he is standing in front of a monument of his father.

"Don't worry father. I will continue your legacy and achieve every single goal you wanted for your kingdom. My methods may be harsher than yours, but that helps us achieve the goal quicker."

Chapter 7

It is a bright, scorching hot day. The sun is shining so bright that it makes everyone's armor look like it is reflecting the sun.

There are armies on both sides of a field. One is Johnathan's army with Charlotte's army beside him.

Johnathan's armor is not on.

Both Johnathan and Charlotte are standing in front of their armies. Both of them and every soldier in the army is equipped and ready to fight.

On the other side is the opposing army. This army looks bigger and even better than their army. It looks bigger and better than both of their armies combined.

The king of this army is named Luis. He looks like a fully grown man with a beard and silver hair. The beard is so long that it actually touches his chest. He is older in age, but he still is a very competent king. He is forty eight years old to be exact.

Jonathan motions to him as if he wants to talk.

All three leaders walk towards each other and meet in the center of the field they are in. However, there is a small bridge that they all stand on that connects the two sides of the field together because there is a small river in between them.

"The golden armored man! It's nice to finally see you in person instead of just hearing rumors about you."

Jonathan just steps into the conversation, "I don't want to negotiate terms. By the looks of things your mind is already made up. You wish to fight. I already know that Kamar offered as much as he wanted to convince you to start a war with me. Therefore, know this, all of you will die here today."

Johnathan's armor turns on.

Luis looks actually a little disappointed. The reason is because of all the rumors he heard he expected him to be a little more mature and thoughtful.

Then he turns his horse around and Johnathan and Charlotte do the same.

As the two of them are riding slowly back to their armies Johnathan turns to Charlotte, "After this battle is over Kamar's biggest supporter will no longer be in our way."

The two of them return back to their armies.

Jonathan is about to give a speech and he is about to open his mouth to speak, but Charlotte gestures to him that she wants to speak. Jonathan lets her.

Charlotte thinks for a moment.

"My brothers in arms! Not all of you will live to see the sunset today! However, I do promise you that by the time this battle is over not only will we be victorious, but we will also never have a fear of Kamar sending his allies to harm us ever again."

She says this speech with great conviction in her voice. As if she has been waiting for this moment for a long time. Charlotte giving this speech restored some of her self-confidence and she can feel that her people have some respect in her restored.

Both armies cheer.

Jonathan looks at her, smiles and nods.

"CHARGE!"

Jonathan shouts at the top of his lungs so loudly that even the armies on the other side can hear it. Therefore, Luis' army charges towards them.

Johnathan's armor immediately turns on.

Both armies are riding towards each other.

While riding together side by side, drawing their swords.

"The king dies last. I want to be the one who kills him. Before I do I want to see the consequences of him taking Kamar's side instead of mine."

As the two armies are getting closer and closer to Luis' army they literally split in half and have one army go to the left while the other goes to the right. It looks as if the two armies are actually trying to box in Luis' army.

Luis realizes what is happening instantly and waves his hand to have his archers start shooting arrows on both sides. The soldiers do of course manage to hit some soldiers and even horses, but it's not enough to break the formation.

Jonathan instantly flies off of his horse and grabs Luis and flies straight up with him.

The soldiers shoot arrows, throw spears, and some even their swords at Johnathan, but it does nothing.

They do end up hitting him, but none of them damage him in any way because the armor is strong for all their weapons.

They literally just bounce off.

Johnathan head butts Luis and this breaks his nose and knocks him out.

Then flies him under the bridge between the two fields.

As soon as he arrives under the bridge the soldiers who are clearly hiding under it immediately start destroying the scaffolding holding the bridge up.

Every single soldier falls under the bridge into the water and the soldiers from Johnathan and Charlotte's armies kill them all one by one.

Johnathan files back up to the field to fight as well.

While fighting he fights very aggressively and ferociously. He fights in a way as if he is taking out his anger on everyone.

As if after all of these feelings like he never really accomplished much is finally being let out.

The war is so bloody and violent that it looks like there is a pig pile of bodies on the field and the grass is being completely repainted from green to red.

Heads being cut off.

Limbs flying all over the place.

Soldiers screaming in agony so loudly that it echoes the field.

Every single soldier is covered in blood and Johnathan's armor looks like it has a red filter on it due to that.

This is the very first time Johnathan has killed people since he has started to help people.

Any other time it came into some sort of conflict with anyone it would be a quick non-fatal fight.

The other way these conflicts would end is by Johnathan injuring someone enough to the point where he knows they won't be a threat anymore.

Killing someone does not affect Johnathan at all. It's not because he does not feel any remorse over it. It's because he feels like killing someone was something that was going to inevitably happen. Even if he tried to avoid it as much as he could.

Luis has been knocked out for a couple of hours. It is the bright rays of the sun that shine onto his face that finally wake him up.

As Luis is waking up he feels very groggy and has quite a headache. However, while he is slowly realizing what is going on he notices that he is not only naked, but that also a lot of his soldiers are killed.

The ones that are still alive are barely hanging on. Because they are losing a lot of blood, or severely injured from the battle.

That thing is though they are not being helped at all. They are actually all being finished off by all of Charlotte's soldiers.

Johnathan is behind the king and slashes him with the sword.

Luis is slashed so hard from behind on his shoulder that it goes through the skin and almost down to his chest.

The blade gets stuck there.

Luis falls right on his face.

The blood spills out of his body and life slowly drains from his eyes.

As this happens his life flashes before his eyes as well.

The main flashes that he sees as the most important moments in his life.

The day he was crowned king.

The day he got married.

The day his wife gave birth to his son.

Finally the day he became an ally with Kamar. The reason this was such an important day for him was because after he became married every single choice he made was to make his life better for his family. Especially after the birth of his son.

He did want what was best for his people, but if it meant that possibly putting his family in danger in any way he would try to find another solution to the problem.

This of course resulted in creation of a lot of tension in his kingdom, but these worries all went to rest when he came to an agreement with Kamar.

Kamar made sure that his family was kept safe and that no one would even think about questioning Luis as Kamar got what he wanted.

That means resources, weapons, or anything he could ever desire.

Which is a big benefit for Kamar because Luis used to have the biggest kingdom at his disposal.

Chapter 8

A red flag with a bear symbol on it goes right over another flag.

A green flag with brown highlights on it. This was the original flag of The Evergreen Dominion. This is the name of the kingdom that Luis gave to it because he constantly used his kingdom to grow and develop more resources.

Suddenly everyone in this kingdom bows before Johnathan.

Although even though the fighting is over his armor does not go away.

"No! I am not your ruler. She is."

Jonathan points right at Charlotte who herself is also covered in blood and tired from all the fighting.

"All hail queen Charlotte!"

The crowd repeats, "All hail queen Charlotte!"

They continue to chat about it over and over.

Charlotte could not help but feel a bit giddy because of the cheering. However, she takes this celebration in with a grain of salt.

There are countless carriages filled with dead bodies. These bodies are from all three armies.

"We brought all the bodies back to bury your dead. We all lost someone today. Take as much as you need to grieve."

Jonathan says this in a very stern but respectful tone in his voice.

"Kamar is not just going to let that loss go. What do we do when he attacks?"

Jonathan responds with a smile on his face, "Walk with me."

She nods and they walk together side by side.

"Also, how am I supposed to rule this kingdom when I still have my own?"

"You will return to your kingdom. Just not yet. I need someone of royal blood to look after this place. Whether it is directly or indirectly. We both agree that just killing Kamar is not enough. Therefore, if we really want to hurt him before killing him we will take away everything that he wants. That has to be done slowly and precisely. Now that we took this kingdom away from him we will rule it in a way he does not want it to be ruled. Instead of using the resources of this place to control people I will bring peace to them. After which the new king or queen will arrive here and I can move onto the next kingdom. When the new ruler is here that's when I'll leave because I need someone to maintain the peace. That's when you can go back home."

Charlotte takes in all that information with a bit of concern. That's because she does not know how long this plan will take to complete.

In a more agitated way, "How are we going to find the next king or queen?"

"We won't have to, you'll make them for me."

Charlotte thinks for a moment and then realizes what Johnathan is talking about.

"No! No! That's not going to happen!"

"I'm not going to force you if you don't want to. However, I think it would be best. Not only to relish in Kamar's anger, but it'll help maintain your density for a longer period of time. Think about it, if you give birth to my child imagine how much more of an advantage they will have."

"You're using me?"

Charlotte snaps right back at him.

"Of course not. This is me just thinking long term. It'll be better if super powered kings continue to rule our kingdoms."

"If I'm in my kingdom, how will I be able to raise a child at the same time? Am I just going to take him with me?"

"Exactly! I will look after this kingdom until the child is ready to the throne for themselves."

After years of psychological torment from Kamar and months and months of creating battle plans to win this war Charlotte finally can actually look towards the future.

Kamar has been this puppeteering voice in her head that has made her choices for her. Not anymore.

Although she does not want to give herself to Johnathan she is going anyway because she feels like she owes him for her freedom. All the while she is slowly winning her people back. Furthermore, having a child with who everyone thinks is a god will help them look upon her more favorably.

She knows the two of them having sex will be inevitable, but she knows she will be uncomfortable because it won't be with Antonio. Therefore, she has to come up with a solution that results in finding some sort of compromise to the situation.

Even Though she does want to come up with a solution to that instantly her gut feeling is telling her she can't think about that right now.

Ever since everyone has been in this kingdom everything just seemed a little too good to be true. They know this has to be some sort of set up.

That's why every single soldier that entered the kingdom they have not settled down yet. They are all actually all on edge.

All the citizens are trying to convince them otherwise.

Offering them food, water, medicine and whatever they need.

No one accepts. Even though there are a bunch of wounded soldiers.

Jonathan and Charlotte have just reached Luis' castle.

The way the two of them know this is by the fact that all the soldiers now look even more on edge and someone can't help but look at a specific tower.

The soldiers look at it as if they are concerned about the fact that Johnathan saw it. Even though of course because some of the spiders keep looking at it makes it even more obvious that something is off.

The tower is not very inconspicuous either. It is painted in dark red with no windows or doors. It looks like it is entirely made out of stone and clearly gives off this sense as if it is trying to protect something.

Jonathan taps Charlotte on the shoulder and points at the tower.

She just notices it.

He picks her up and flies towards the tower.

The speed towards the tower is great but when he hits it he does not break through. He ends up just making a crack in it.

This sound the hit made was so loud and rough that this gets the attention of literally everyone in the kingdom. Plus creating a mini earthquake.

The soldiers in Evergreen attack all of the soldiers of Jonathan and Charlotte's armies.

The soldiers around the tower start throwing all of their spears at Johnathan. While others shoot arrows at him.

Every single one of Luis' soldiers in this kingdom is now in panic mode to try to stop Johnathan.

Since he is holding Charlotte in his hand he has to block all these attacks towards him to not accidentally hit Charlotte.

"Hold on to me!"

Jonathan shouts this as he flies a little further back and forth towards the tower.

Hitting again and again until he actually starts to dent it. To the point where he can see a small little hole in it. He then starts punching that hole to make it bigger.

At this point faint crying can be heard in the tower. It is unclear whose cry it is, but this does get Johnathan a little excited because he assumes it is Kamar.

Then eventually he starts to pull the stones apart to where he can make an opening big enough for him and Charlotte to enter.

The punches end up making dents in the armor.

The faint crying turns to loud sobbing.

They both immediately notice there is a woman in here and no one else.

When the two of them get in the tower the soldiers don't stop, they continue to attack.

"Everyone to that tower now!"

A random soldier shouts from the group so loudly that the two of them can hear it.

In the tower there is a woman who is cradled in a position as if she is trying to protect something.

This is Sydney.

She is dressed in royal clothes and a crown on her head.

Both of them just stop what they are doing and realize they made a mistake.

The woman slowly turns around and the crying continues. She is holding a small baby boy in her arms. The baby's name is Joshua.

Both Johnathan and Charlotte put their arms up and slowly back away as if they don't mean any harm to her or the baby.

"You killed my husband and now you are going to take over the kingdom. How can you expect me not to think of you as a threat?"

Jonathan cuts in, "We are here to make things better for everyone."

"THEN WHERE WERE YOU FOR THE PAST THREE WEEKS?"

Sydney barks right back at him.

Charlotte is incredibly confused by what was just said.

"Three weeks? The war was only one week ago. What other lies has Kamar told you?"

Chapter 9

As the days pass by in Evergreen there is this sense of reassurance in the land.

The first step that was done to help everyone in the kingdom feel that is by killing all of Kamar's spies.

Sydney and Johnathan start to get along better because Johnathan stays true to his word.

He helps Sydney take care of his son, look after the kingdom and help maintain this feeling of reassurance.

People are not only happy here, but also very united with each other.

All the while Johnathan and Charlotte keep sleeping together until she gets pregnant.

Every time Charlotte and Johnathan sleep together she has to think of Antonio. That is the only way that she can enjoy it because in her mind she was never going to ever sleep with anyone else besides Antonio.

All the same time whenever they do sleep together Johnathan has this sense of hoping he performs well. That is not because this is the first woman he has slept with, but because he always has this need of always wanting to feel like he is making people's lives better. He always over-thinks sex. To make sure that Charlotte is pleased.

One night while everyone is asleep Sydney goes to Luis' grave.

She is holding the baby in her hands while it is sleeping.

She looks at the grave with sadness, but she does not cry.

"I just wanted to come by and say, 'hello.' Thank you for everything, my love. We are both doing well, as matter of fact, better than before. I know you are a big contributor to that, however, I know you would be upset at what I am about to do. Therefore, this is why I came here to tell you that from now on everyone will think that the baby is not yours, but his. If this is what it takes to keep our family safe I will do it. Plus Johnathan wants to share all of our other resources with every other kingdom. Our elected officials are clearly not happy about this, but from what I've seen Johnathan do I have to just put my faith in him. He will not disappoint."

First thing as soon as the sun rises Johnathan and Charlotte go into the hot tub just to relax.

"It's so frustrating that it's taking so long to get pregnant. I need to get back," Charlotte barks.

"I know. Hopefully soon," Jonathan responds gently.

"The second I get pregnant I'm leaving. If you ever want to see me or the child you are coming there," her voice sounds a little more agitated now.

"I feel like this goes without saying," Jonathan says in a reassuring way.

Suddenly a bunch of guards barge in with swords and shields as if they are ready to fight. There are five of them to be exact.

Jonathan's armor immediately turns on and he fights them all off.

Due to all the commotion Charlotte runs out of the hot tub, gets minimally dressed and gets her soldiers.

Jonathan fights with his hands and hurts all of the soldiers a lot. Three of them are passed out, while one has his jaw dislocated from the punches, and the final one has a couple of broken bones. This puts that one into enough shock.

Jonathan is very out of breath, "I don't want to kill anyone today so just tell me who sent you and I will spare your lives!"

At that moment the others arrive. Ten of Charlotte's soldiers, fully armored, are there with weapons.

A random soldier says out of desperation, "Every member of the political council!"

"Lock them all up. You two put them in a cell. The rest of you follow me!"

Jonathan states this sentence in a very growly way.

All the politicians are having a meeting and then Johnathan shoots through the wooden door as if it was nothing.

All of them are completely shaken up because of this.

"Which one of you fuckers tried to have me killed?"

All the political counselors look at each other as if they are trying to blame each other.

Instantly they are all taken away and arrested.

Back in his bedroom he checks in on Charlotte to make sure she is safe.

Sydney runs into the room after hearing about what happened.

"Tell me you're going to have them all executed?"

Sydney says very instinctively as if she is not thinking about the words that she let out of her mouth.

"No. I don't know what to do yet." Jonathan says in an inconsistent tone.

Sydney instantly replies, "What do you mean you don't know? They tried to kill you. The BOTH of you. If I was you I would kill them then and there. Without trial or arresting them or any kind of due process."

Jonathan responds gently, "I don't want to show the people that I'm a tyrannical king. I'm trying to build a world that is better than Kamar's. Therefore, I will show them mercy."

Sydney and Charlotte, "WHAT?"

Jonathan puts his hands up in a reassuring way.

"I'm just going to have them be exiled. They will be left out there in the wilderness to fend for themselves if starvation does not kill them, then some sort of animal will. Even though I won't kill them. I will make an example of them."

"You do realize that if they get another chance they will try to kill you again?"

There is a blatantly clear condescending tone to her question.

"Obviously! That's why I'm not keeping them in this kingdom. If by any chance they could possibly escape their cell or if they have any other allies trying to help them we can stop it," Jonathan barks right back at her.

The next day all of the council members are standing in the middle of Evergreen. All of the soldiers that were attacking Johnathan and Charlotte are there too. As well as any other allies that they have.

All of them have no clothes on and walk through the city to the front gates in shame.

Everyone is shaming them by throwing food at them, swearing, spitting on them, or any other kind of despicable thing that can possibly be done.

Once they reach the gate they are literally just let go into the world without any kind of aid.

Jonathan is standing at the center of the front gate watching them leave with Charlotte on his right and Sydney on his left.

Sydney suddenly turns around and faces the people, "Let that be a warning to anyone who decides to go after my family!"

Jonathan and Charlotte both look at her kind of shocked.

Over the next couple of weeks Johnathan's goals finally get achieved.

Peace is achieved indirectly because of the fear tactic that was used by Johnathan. Everyone is just too scared to do anything out of fear of getting exiled. On top of that everyone who is imprisoned at this point is never allowed out, even if they served their sentence. To simply not risk them becoming reoffenders.

All the while, Jonathan finally gets Charlotte pregnant.

The moment she realizes this she goes back home to her kingdom.

Jonathan escorts her back along with all of the soldiers in Charlotte's army.

Chapter 10

A random soldier's head has just been cut off.

"Can no one figure out a goddamn solution to killing the son of a bitch? 'The Iron God,' as people are calling him now."

Kamar says this as he has a sword in his hand and slowly walks back to a servant that has a tray of grapes on it. He grabs them and starts eating them one by one.

There are actually several dead bodies here. All of them with their heads cut off and blood all over the place.

His hair looks a lot longer. It actually touches his shoulders. Plus he is slightly grown in height. Therefore, he clearly has aged.

However, only a year. He is now eleven years old.

Kamar continues to rant, "All though no one talks about the fact that he has caused a bunch of fear in people. A fear of war in particular. All of a sudden one day he may just attack their kingdom and take what he wants in the name of 'peace.' Give me a break. Plus does that sound very reliable? One king to rule the world. Even I understand that when I achieved that goal I needed to do it from the background. That's why I needed someone to be in the foreground. Someone who actually knew what they were doing. King, politicians, generals and so on. I'm not just some guy who has a savior complex."

There is a guard that runs right up to Kamar and whispers in his ear, "The twin kings of Bartholomew and Nathanael are here to visit you. 'We need your help, urgently.' That was the message they wanted me to pass on to you."

Kamar nods, "send them in."

Both of them enter, with all of their soldiers too. The color scheme of the twins and their army is black and white. Split right down the middle the armor of the soldiers is black and white. Including the royal clothes and the twins.

Nathaniel and Bartholomew are a pair of twin brothers. Both of them look Caucasian. They are both thirty years old and really tall men. Both are six feet and two inches tall both with blonde hair and water blue eyes.

They all instantly fall to their knees and bow to him.

Nathaniel has an incredible sense of desperation in his voice, "we need your help, my lord."

"I'm listening..."

Kamar says this in a very stoic tone. Bartholomew is looking around at the dead bodies, and he suddenly gets grossed out.

He puts his hand over his mouth and nose to shield himself from the smell.

Nathaniel continues, "We've thought of a plan on how to stop Goldman. It's a full proof plan that no matter the outcome you will be able to take everything back that was stolen from you."

Bartholomew, "and we can finally control all the chaos that is going in our kingdom."

Kamar appears to listen but has the attitude as if the words he is hearing is in one ear out the other.

"Why have you gone to James before me? I thought you guys were friends."

Nathaniel scoffs, "we're only friends with him when his queen lets us be friends. Therefore, I think he would be very unreliable in achieving this goal. You're the only one we can count on."

Kamar has this look on his face of accepted disappointment, "all right. Let's talk. If the plan makes no sense you're joining my collection of headless corpuses."

All of Kamar's spies all over every single kingdom are gone and they come back to Sodom.

All the while Kamar shares all of his resources with the twins. This results in more of a sense of balance in both kingdoms.

Back at Solstice Charlotte has just given birth.

Although Johnathan is not there. He is in Eden at this point making plans to take over the next kingdom.

At this point Johnathan is eighteen years old. He has gotten a haircut to remove all of his hair. His whole eyes are now gold as well. Not just his pupil. He has grown even taller; he is now seven foot 2 inches.

While Eden is still maintaining peace there is a clear loss of direction for this kingdom. The reason is because they have no consistent ruler in their kingdom. Therefore, to make sure that there is a ruler that is consistent Johnathan decides to get another woman pregnant here too.

Therefore, he stays in Eden until that happens.

Eventually he ends up getting a woman pregnant. That's the moment he leaves and goes back to Solstice.

When he arrives back there everyone is cheering for him as he flies through the skies.

Upon arriving at Charlotte's quarters he enters them very quietly. Charlotte is there with a couple of servants to help take care of the baby. It is a baby boy whose name is Oliver.

Charlotte looks exactly the same as the last time Johnathan saw her. Just slightly taller.

Jonathan is at a loss for words. He is very shaken up by the fact that he officially became a dad.

Charlotte whispers, "I wonder if he will have any powers like you."

Jonathan whispers back to her, "I guess we'll have to wait and see. My powers did not start showing up until I was ten years old. So when are you letting me take him to Evergreen?"

Charlotte instantly tenses up, "about that? I don't think that should happen."

Jonathan raises his eyebrow, "excuse me?"

"You didn't think you'd just show up after months of not seeing us and then suddenly I'd just let you take him from me."

She clearly has a very trembling tone in her voice. The reason is because this instantly triggers her is because of the fact that standing up to someone is something new for her. Furthermore, whenever she did it before there would be bad consequences for it.

Jonathan collects his words for a moment, "I'm just confused. We agreed to this beforehand."

Charlotte clearly gets a little more irritated, "I know. There is something that at the time I think both of us did consider. Which is the fact that one day I'm going to die. When that happens I need someone who looks after the kingdom, no?"

Jonathan looks completely dumb founded.

"I feel so stupid. How could I not think of this? I need some time to think."

Charlotte nods as Johnathan flies away.

He flies around with no sense of direction. It's just him and his thoughts flowing through his brain as the clouds continue to flow throughout the night sky.

All the while back at Sodom they are preparing for war.

Stronger weapons are being made.

Furthermore, literally every single person in this kingdom is working.

Kamar is in his bedroom just eating food. He looks quite disgusting. He has a decent sized belly at this point and eats food off of himself.

The reason he is acting like this is out of pure anxiety. He is afraid of being forgotten. Whether or not he ends up getting killed in the war with Johnathan, how long until he is erased.

There is a knock on the front door.

"Come in."

A messenger enters with a letter in her hands.

"From the twins, your majesty."

The messenger hands him the letter and sits there and waits for him to read it.

"My lord, I apologize for taking so long to reach out to you. My wife has just given birth to my daughter, and my brother has just figured out his wife was pregnant. Everything is going according to plan. We've built some new and stronger weapons. We think we can actually end up breaking Johnathan's armor because of it."

Kamar suddenly gets an epiphany. To have as many children as possible to continue his dynasty. Whether he is here or not to see it grow.

Kamar looks over at the messenger. "Can you please close the door behind you? I need your help with something."

Jonathan's direct flight led him back to Evergreen.

He sees Sydney and Joshua just playing.

He lands near them. He waves, 'hello' to the both of them.

Jonathan is just there watching the both of them play.

Sydney walks towards him and kills his shoulder.

Suddenly Joshua, who is only ten months and a half at this point crawls over to him trying to hand him a toy.

"Dada..."

Sydney giggles with excitement.

Jonathan could not help, but smile as well. However, suddenly he has this sense of clarity.

He knows for a fact he can't assume that people are going to do what he wants them to do. Furthermore, it does not matter whether these people are adults or kids they could not be forced to make decisions they don't want to make. Although, if he has a bunch of children then he can teach them how to rule the kingdom using the rules and laws that Johnathan established.

Chapter 11

Over the next five years things are pretty peaceful throughout all the kingdoms.

Even though Kamar is still preparing for war he has had a lot of children within that time period. Thirty-two specifically and another on the way. Three kids with eleven mothers. All the kids range from under six months to almost five years old. They are all born in Sodom, but are of many different ethnicities.

He does not have any time to raise or educate the children in any way. Therefore, the mothers of the children and all the servants help raise and educate them.

The main reason he does not educate them is because even though he is only sixteen years old at this point, he wants his strategy for what happens to his dynasty after his death to be set in stone.

Johnathan is floating over the main gate of the next kingdom he has to take over. Marshville. Which is also the name of the dynasty of this kingdom.

Below him there is a small army with no more than one hundred men.

At twenty-three years old Johnathan has grown even more to eight feet tall. His armor has changed a shade slightly. It also has become very shiny to the point where you can use the armor as a mirror.

Jonathan shoots through the front gate and all his men enter the kingdom.

The kingdom looks completely deserted.

They walk through the whole thing as if there is not a single living thing in here.

The flag of this kingdom is a black spider with a red background.

However, the color scheme of everything else in the kingdom such as the buildings, landscape and overall look of it is very inconsistent. The color scheme of this place looks like it is constantly changing. This is made very clear by the fact that a bunch of colors look smudged together.

All the soldiers including Johnathan do have all their weapons drawing thinking this must be a trap.

They eventually end up at this building where when they enter it looks like an arena.

Suddenly fires get lit and drumming starts beating, and cheering is heard.

A woman is seen sitting in a chair with a front row view of the arena.

"Welcome ladies and gentlemen and boys and girls! To the fight of the century!"

The annoying voice comes from Marsha. The queen of the kingdom. She is a darker skin toned woman with orange hair. She appears to be of Indian descent. She has a taller and slimmer build and is thirty-five years old.

"Let us hear it for the Golden Giant, everyone!"

Everyone cheers and cheers louder and louder.

All the soldiers get ready to fight.

Another man enters the arena from the opposite end of them. This is James. The king of the kingdom. He is also of Indian descent with blonde hair. He is also very tall as well. He is six foot three and half to be exact. He is covered in armor from head to toe. He also has multiple weapons on him to the point where he looks like a one man army.

"What the hell is going on here?"

The shire confusion can be heard in his voice even though his mask is on.

James barks back, "tell your soldiers to back down. This is between you and me."

"I'm not doing anything until I know what's going on."

Marsha cuts in, "It's a battle to the death! We've heard stories of the Golden God for years now and we knew it was only a matter of time before you tried to invade our kingdom so we wanted to be ready. That being said, the more stories I heard about you the more interesting they became. Therefore, I came up with an offer. If my husband wins he takes everything that belongs to you. If you win you get everything that belongs to him."

"This makes no sense."

James shouts at him, "Hey! Would you rather do this or the body count being in the hundreds?"

Jonathan nods at his soldiers and they do just that.

The two of them start to fight.

While the two of them fight Marsha has a clear look of arousal on her face to the simple fact there are two men fighting over her.

The two of them are fighting very skillfully and proficiently.

At the same time though James seems to be the one who is the more aggressive out of the two of them.

The main reason this is happening is because he is taking out his resentment on Jonathan.

This resentment that James has comes from Marsha. Even though she is his queen and even though they have been married for a long time it was not a good marriage.

She is the queen of her own kingdom, but she has to be the best queen of every kingdom. She is not an entitled person in the sense that she thinks she wants to be the best queen in the world. She wants to be the queen who has the best in the world. The best king, the best citizens, the best food, the best of everything. That results in her doing a lot of things that are clearly very selfish. She sleeps around, screws people over, and steals and cheats in any way she can so she can get the best.

The thing is though even after she got married to James she did not stop this. Therefore, this resulted in a lot of tension with the king and his kingdom plus a lot of spite towards Marsha from James.

He eventually was able to get her to calm down on her greedy side. Due to the fact that James was a push over a lot of the politicians in the city try to get Marsha killed. Once he told her from being poisoned she calmed down. However, that being said she still tried whatever she wanted and manipulated and used James in her own selfish way.

James went with it if it meant building back trust in him and the people. That's because at this point he and Marsha came to a mutual understanding. She can do whatever she wants, but she has to console James. That way James can protect her in any way he can and at the same time make sure she does not cross too big a line to keep this sense of trust with the people.

While in the arena the two of them have been fighting for a solid ten minutes and the audience is riveted.

Eventually Johnathan gets the better of James by stabbing him in the knee. Then stabs him through the chin to the brain from a knife.

After killing him he takes a step back and breathes a sigh of relief.

"Congratulations to the new KING!"

Everyone is cheering nonstop and Marsha is clapping too.

Jonathan's armor goes away, "that was easy."

Marsha eventually gets to the center stage herself and immediately rushes up to Johnathan and kisses him.

She has her eyes on clothes and tries to kiss him passionately. He is just confused.

He pulls her away abruptly.

"What are you doing?"

"Kissing my new husband."

"Excuse me?"

"Well, you won the fight therefore you get everything he owned. Including me."

"Shouldn't you be in mourning?"

"Why? I get the next best thing."

Just like that Johnathan continues to accept her advances.

Chapter 12

Kamar is on a horse in front of his army. Nathanael and Bartholomew are on the right and left side of their horses. Kamar is now twenty years old and the twins are in their forties. Kamar is now also five foot ten.

Jonathan is in front of his army. However, not on a horse, but levitating in front of it.

Right below is Charlotte. She has grown to five foot eight. Also, she looks bigger. In a more muscular way. She is not bulky, but much fit.

Both Johnathan and Charlotte are in their mid-twenties at this point.

Behind both of them is an army in the millions. All of the soldiers have different colored armor, weapons and shields.

They are all here to fight.

This is the final stand.

Jonathan pulls out his sword and Kamar does the same.

Charlotte does the same.

They both shout at the top of their lungs, "CHARGE!"

As both armies run towards each other Johnathan lowers himself closer to the ground.

However, the closer Johnathan and Charlotte get to the opposing army the more Kamar lets himself get swallowed into the army. This ends up giving him the ability to hide in the army.

As the armies finally meet and clash together and begin fighting.

A bunch of the soldiers further back in Kamar's army shoot arrows aimlessly. Sometimes hitting people sometimes not. These arrows are very special; they are metal arrows made out of the same material as the swords they are using. This metal is stronger than any of the armor that all of Johnathan's soldiers are wearing.

Therefore, a lot of dead bodies from one side of the field then the other.

Kamar's men are slowly catching up to that number though.

Through the entire fight both Johnathan and Charlotte are looking for Kamar.

Jonathan can't seem to find him no matter how hard he tries.

Therefore, he takes out his anger in the fight as much as he can.

The soldiers bring out a very big bow and arrow like machine.

It is huge. The arrow itself looks like it is twelve feet long. With this machine being thirty feet high and fifty feet wide. There are three of these machines.

They fire the first arrow at Jonathan. It misses and hits a group of five people. It goes through all of them.

The others are fired right after. Both hit Johnathan. It knocks the wind right out of him. These arrows are hard enough to create more detents in his armor. One arrow hits hard enough that the dent it made hit Johnathan's skin that it bruised him.

Charlotte notices this and runs towards him.

"Protect the king!"

Charlotte gets a handful of soldiers and they make a circle around him.

Eventually Bartholomew and Nathanael step forward.

Both of them fight Charlotte and she can hold her own.

Clearly though the more the fight goes on she clearly feels overwhelmed.

The twins end up killing all the other soldiers that were around Johnathan.

Therefore, Bartholomew continues to fight her while Nathanael stands over Johnathan trying to destroy the armor.

He clearly can't because it appears as if the armor is attached to him.

Eventually he ends up collecting himself again, using his wings to block the sword. This results in Nathaniel dropping his sword. Johnathan grabs Nathaniel's sword and stabs him in the side with it.

Bartholomew is distracted by this for just enough time that Charlotte cuts his throat.

Jonathan gets back up and continues to fight with Charlotte back to back.

The more the battle goes on and Johnathan realizes that they are going to win.

This results in the chaos calming down slightly. Therefore, they are a couple of people who try to run away.

Jonathan takes note of that and flies right over to the horses to find Kamar.

When they find Kamar he looks at Johnathan with complete contempt.

He spits in his face. Jonathan brings Kamar back to Johnathan.

Charlotte has a great look of anger and disgust on her face.

"No matter how badly I want to kill you right here and now I can't do that. It is too easy. You will be executed soon enough, but not until I hear you beg for it."

Jonathan then adds on, "all your soldiers will be killed, no one will be spared. Enjoy every moment you have left of being a king because it is going to be over soon."

As Johnathan is talking, all of Kamar's soldiers along with the twins' soldiers are all killed off. No one is spread and no mercy is shown.

Chapter 13

Kamar is in a cage with chains holding him down.

Jonathan, Charlotte and every surviving soldier got back to Eden.

Every single person is cheering.

Kamar is taken to a tower. This tower looks like a torture chamber.

"Specifically made for you," utters Johnathan.

That line gives Kamar so many goosebumps that it is the first in his entire life he knew that there will be nothing to save him.

For the next several months he is tortured non-stop. He is whipped, beaten, and has done countless unimaginable things to him by both Charlotte and Johnathan.

Eventually he is executed by Charlotte. However, he is not killed in Eden.

The two of them take Kamar back to Sodom. He is once again in a cage, tied down with chains.

He is taken to the exact center of the kingdom with everyone in it surrounding it.

Jonathan and Charlotte dig a hole right in front of him.

"Any last words?" Charlotte utters in a very snarky way.

Kamar shakes his head. However, he barely has any energy and his body is so badly scared that he is barely recognizable.

They bring him out of the cage and sit him down right in front of the hole.

Charlotte cuts his head clean off and kicks the body into the hole.

Everyone is screaming and terrified.

Jonathan cuts in, "YOUR KING HAS JUST BEEN DEFEATED BY YOUR NEW RULERS!"

Out of pure fear everyone just bows.

For the next couple of weeks they stay in Sodom to clean this place up.

Jonathan does this all alone even though Charlotte wanted to help.

All of the spies that Kamar has in his kingdom and all over the world are killed off.

The wealth of the kingdom is distributed a lot more equally for everyone. This is accomplished a lot quicker because of the fact that he shares the resources from Evergreen to here.

After staying in Sodom for a year because he feels like it was "fixed" enough he goes to the final kingdom to finally achieve his goal.

The twins' kingdom is called Geaman. This is the kingdom that is the most chaotic out of all the others he has seen before. The main reason is because after the final battle with Kamar and the twins, Geaman was completely abandoned. Therefore, everyone there did not have a leader so they did whatever was needed to survive. It resulted in all the royalty being killed off by the citizens. The kingdom ran out of food and water and every other resource needed. Even the children in this kingdom are affected by the chaos and they get violent because of it.

The second Johnathan arrives at Geaman and sees all the chaos, something in him just snaps and he decides to just kill almost everyone. This feeling came from a great sense of panic because he is so close to achieving his goal that he just wants it over with.

He is here completely alone. No soldiers or back up of any kind.

This ends up almost getting him killed because there are so many people. Even though he does have his armor on its not indestructible therefore, there is the occasional person that gets a lucky shot that does hurt him.

He literally looks repainted in blood and guts by the end of the fight. This entire kingdom looks like it is hell on earth. The only ones that are spared are people who swore themselves to Johnathan as king.

His goal is finally complete.

Chapter 14

Within a year of achieving his goal world peace is achieved.

All the people that were appointed by Johnathan to lead the other kingdoms worked.

Everyone is working together to help keep this sense of peace.

Even though everyone is not happy about the way things are being run, not many people are complaining because it worked.

Ironically, one of the people in the world who is not happy about this is Johnathan. He has actually become quite bitter even though everything is working out in his favor. Besides peace being achieved, all the kids he has have superhuman abilities that are either similar to his or something completely different from his. The powers that are different are very fantastical. Such as super human strength, teleportation, super speed, the ability to shoot lighting out of their hands and countless others. Everyone else seems to be doing well and no one has a fear of being attacked.

The main reason he is very bitter is because he feels like he has no purpose now.

Peace has defeated it.

Therefore, he looks for countless other reasons to stop other bad things from happening. The problem is he's not stepping in when he needs to, he is stepping in when he suspects a problem.

For example, one day when he randomly just flies around he sees two people being really aggressive towards each other. . He flies right now to them and hits them both hard enough that it knocks them out in one punch.

"You're welcome," Jonathan utters.

Those two words are said in a way as if he not only fixed a problem, but also got everyone to stop focusing on the two of them. Even though no one was listening and actually everyone was looking at him and the two people knocked out now.

He continues to do this for years and even decades. Looking for problems to fix. Crimes to stop. Unfortunately also for people to beat on. He is so focused on this that he does not pay attention to the bigger picture.

Such as people slowly starting rebellions. The queens that gave birth to his children become distant. He is completely absent from the children and neglectful of the people around him. To the point where small rebellions are being formed in each kingdom.

As he continues to age it shows a lot on him physically. He ages just like any other person. However, his abilities are affected too.

His wings start to lose feathers to the point where he can't really fly as high or as further anymore. Furthermore, his army is weaker. To the point that bits of can get damaged a lot easier and actually fall off as well. Which makes him a lot more vulnerable.

Therefore, the less he is able to do physically.

By the time he reached the age of sixty he stopped fighting and helping people in the way he usually would.

He helps people in a different way. He passes on all of his knowledge. Whether his fighting techniques, his mind set, how his powers work, or even just talking about his experiences. It's not always the wisest information or the worded in the best way, but it does help a lot of people. It's mainly educating them in some way.

He also does this for twenty years. At ninety years of age where his wings are practically gone and the armor is completely gone he is laying on his deathbed.

Back in Eden.

He looks incredibly wrinkly and has very little hair, very little teeth and a fragile and frail looking physique.

The entire world is mourning for him. Around his deathbed there are a bunch of people around him taking up the entire space of the room. These are all his children, and more of them are outside the castle too.

All of the women he has had kids with are here. The ones that are still alive.

As Johnathan gasps his last breath he looks in front of him and sees all of the children with superpowers and all the goals he achieved and smiles.

PART 2

THE GATEKEEPERS

Chapter 15

I don't know what's happening to me, but I don't like it.

I know I'm dead because I'm looking at my lifeless corpse. While everyone continues to cry around me.

Something is pulling me up, but I don't know what. I'm trying to swim back towards my body, but I'm stuck. Mentally I want to move. However, physically I can't.

I'm tugging on like a puppet on strings. The only direction I'm moving in is up.

Eventually I got up to a very purple looking light. Once I pass through it I can actually look at myself. It looks like my physical form looks very abnormal. I'm covered in the same golden color as my armor, but I'm not in my armor. It's like I'm just floating like a feather.

The purple light led me to another location that is nothing like I've seen before. Everything is colored in purple except these glass like mirrors that I can see at a distance.

The most bizarre thing about the entire situation is that whenever I float past one of these mirrors I can see my reflection. However, it is a different version of me.

The differences are monumental. Skin color, eye color, and even a complete body type. The most noticeable thing is that I can see myself with different abilities.

These abilities appear to be so much more fantastic than my flight and armored powers. As I try to reach for them it feels as if something is literally holding me back from doing it.

I've continued to float through this place for who knows how long, but finally I reached a mirror where I can actually reach out and touch.

In this mirror my reflection looks gold once again. However, it does not look like armor. It's as if this is my actual skin. Also, I don't have any wings in it either. However, I can still fly just without wings.

Instantly though I could help, but I felt freaked out. I pull out my arm and try to push myself away. Unfortunately, just like before I can't. As a matter of fact I was pushed into it.

Then from the purple colors I see a bright light. Then suddenly pitch black. Not the color, but literally black. Nothing. A dark endless void.

I'm clearly stuck in this void for a long time, because the longer I'm here the more cramped I feel. It's as if I'm forced to be in an uncomfortable position.

Then suddenly another light is seen.

I'm suddenly out of this uncomfortable position. I can move slightly. However, not much. I'm trying to speak, but can't. I'm only making noises.

"It's a healthy baby boy, but why is he gold? One voice says.

"Oh no. The bleeding is not stopping!" Another voice yells.

Everyone sounds very frantic.

I can understand what is happening around me. I remember all of my memories. Why do I keep getting passed around from person to person?

UNBELIEVABLE!

I'm a new born baby.

Everyone is running around trying to save the woman who gave birth to me. At least that's what I think is happening. I'm not sure I keep getting passed around.

I get taken into another room and a woman who looks like a house maid is changing me.

Then suddenly a man comes in who is dressed in royal clothes with a crown on top of his head. He looks furious at me.

The look on his face is fury that is slowly slipping away, but he does not want to let it go. Then it breaks, he gets sad, then cries then that face turns into remorse.

Chapter 16

Why am I in Sodom? How much time has passed since I died?

These are questions that unfortunately I can't get any answers to due to the fact that I can't talk yet. I guess I won't get answers the old fashioned way. I guess the only way I can do that is by observing everyone.

The first thing that I noticed is that the second I was born, everyone's mood changed. Especially when they were around me.

Even though I'm only a baby they are clearly looking at me as if I'm someone special. I'm guessing that they are making sure that I am happy with what they are doing?

Making sure they are still following the laws I created?

At the age of six what they want to see is what my powers are. The ability to fly was found really quickly. I was simply just thrown off of the roof of the tallest castle in Sodom and eventually I stopped falling and started levitating.

When it came to the strength of the armor that was a test of trial and error. They were able to figure out very quickly that the armor was different in the sense that it could not just go away. The obvious observation is the fact that no matter what my mood was, the armor was always on. What was the most bizarre part about the armor was the fact that it made a perfect textured outline of my body. Every single muscle is outlined as if my body is being put on display. Every single muscle is outlined to the most perfect detail.

Once I am able to speak properly and I can finally have conversations with people everything seems too good to be true.

Everyone tells me whatever I need to hear. It's just too perfect. I don't buy it. Where are all my kids? Charlotte? Sydney? The biggest question of all: why didn't any of them come to visit me once they knew I was back?

The moon is shining bright and everyone is asleep. I will go up and away from this kingdom to see how the rest of the world is doing.

I continue to fly higher and higher and the walls never end. Eventually I had to stop and go back down because I could not breathe properly. As a matter of fact I still felt like I was going to pass out.

I ended up landing back on the ground in a very clumsy way.

When school started I felt like this perfect was becoming much more nonsensical.

Especially all the history classes. They would talk about all the things I achieved and they were incorrect. Not the events themselves, but how those events happened.

When I finally confronted my teacher one day in school about it she told me that, "some of these facts might be false. That's because they happened over one hundred years ago. How can we possibly know exactly how they happened? Especially things that happened to someone else. Also, you can't just sit there and tell me you have a perfect memory and that you can recall everything that happened to the exact detail. Right?"

The weird thing was that my teacher sounded really hostile.

So information is also being held from me on purpose? What the fuck is going on here?

The next day that teacher is gone. No one knows where she is apparently. It's as if she just vanished. Throughout this entire day at school everyone got upset with me about the teacher leaving. I could not help, but feel some sort of guilt because of it. I was just trying to help not make things worse.

The more I try the more upset people get. Probably the best thing for me to do is to just submit.

Let's see what happens.

It's just hit my one hundred and twelfth birthday. Twenty-second, technically, if I'm just counting the years of this life. Also, I just reached the height of eight feet tall.

Everyone in this kingdom helps me celebrate it. Even the king of Sodom, Boren. Along with his daughter Bella. She is twenty years old and of mixed race. Both Caucasian and Latino.

Boren is the king of Sodom now instead of me. The reason is because since I did submit myself to the kingdom becoming king would contradict that. Furthermore, this is better for everyone since they like him more than me. I've also had no problems with him myself so I don't see why he can't be trusted.

After submitting myself to the rules of the kingdom things have become easier. This is why everyone is helping me celebrate my birthday. There is this great sense of satisfaction throughout the kingdom. I know I have something to do with that because I am helping improve this kingdom. From passing on my knowledge to them they were able to use it to create new inventions to help others. Such as creating a new form of transportation that doesn't require horses.

While we are all celebrating my birthday Bella suddenly comes up to me and hugs me. Then whispers in my ear, "I'm pregnant."

That was unexpected. However, as much as I'd like to talk to her more about this, I can't right now. Not because of the party but because of the fact that no one knows we're together. Not even her father. We started sleeping together when she was eighteen and I just turned twenty. To be honest I'm really surprised that this happened because I already had so many kids that I didn't want anymore. Plus I'm hoping to see some of them again soon.

The next day as Bella and I are going for a walk together I get randomly punched by someone. Of course this does not hurt me at all because of my metal golden texture, but this instantly breaks this citizen's hand.

It is clear that Bella recognizes him, but acts like she doesn't.

"Guards! Guards! We need help!" Bella shouts this as if her life depends on it.

Guards run up to the man, they take him instantly away and Bella takes my hand and walks in the opposite direction.

"Who is that?"

"What? Oh, no one."

"Don't lie to me, Bella."

"I'm not. I don't know him. Maybe his face looks familiar due to the fact that I've seen him several times throughout the kingdom before, but I don't know him personally."

No matter how I try to push for her to give me an honest answer she won't. I want to push further, but the more I push the more guards around me look like they are ready to attack me. Therefore, I back down to not make the situation worse.

Suddenly my eyes shoot open as I can feel that someone is standing right over me. King Boren is standing right over me. He has this death stare. We got figured out.

"We were going to tell you…" I utter with a bit of concern in my voice.

"I'm not talking about that."

His eyes have not shifted away from me.

"You got my daughter killed. Since you were born I wanted to kill you. As payback for killing my wife. I started thinking long term. If we can do as much as we can even to make Sodom better. Even if it means using my daughter to give me a super powered dynasty.…"

I cut him off instantly, "wait what? You knew that we were together?"

Boren suddenly has this smug look on his face, "of course. It was my idea in the first place."

The moment he said that I instantly stood up on the bed and started to levitate on the bed. I pull away to the point where I can stand up and look like I am just floating in the air straight up. I felt really hurt by what happened because I thought it was real. However, I feel dumb as to why I even fell for that?

"How did she die?"

"She was stabbed to death by some locals. Apparently she was together before with one of them. You don't have to worry about it. We 'arrested' them like the rest."

I bark at him, "Arrest them? Why didn't you just kill them?"

Boren sighs and continues, "you really haven' realized what has happened over the past twenty years?"

I feel like I already did figure it out, but I'll play into his hand.

"What are you talking about?"

"You oblivious buffoon. HA! The great Golden Phoenix could not figure out that he was being groomed! Everything around is FAKE! To just keep you from starting a third world war. After you conquered the entire world we took it back. Kamar has countless kids of his own. All of them raised to take back and fight for Sodom and the world to continue Kamar's dynasty. If that meant eventually having to kill all your allies, even your kids so be it. Everything was fine for a while but then when you were born we had to figure out a way to shut you off from the truth. Deception on a global level achieved that goal. Fake relationships. Friendships. Alternating history to make you think everything was perfect. Take away any kind of cause that could lead to the effect of a crime. If you ask me it was for the better. The moment you died everyone in the world fought over you in terms of who should be number one. We honestly thought the world was going to tear itself apart. However, we took back control of it in the end."

Every word that comes out of his mouth makes me angrier and angrier. More than anything, my facial expressions say it all. At the same time it's good that it got him to spell his guts to me.

"Bella?"

"Simple. We needed to pass on the bloodline and we knew that you liked her. Therefore, we wanted to take advantage of the opportunity to have our superhuman children that were going to be raised by us. Then we would have a better dynasty without and eventually a better world. The unfortunate thing is it took some a long time to persuade her. That's because she did not like you back. She liked that man whose wrist broke because he hit you. Apparently that's what stopped her from going along with the plan. Eventually she gave in for spite towards me. She thought that what was going to happen is that after giving birth to your child she was just going to queen and not worry about me getting in the way. While you just take off your kid and she goes off with the guy."

I raise myself up in flight as if I'm going to attack.

"I guess that all doesn't matter now that she's dead. Therefore, what's the point of keeping you around?"

Boren has his hand on the grip of his sword, about to draw the sword. I fly at him with full speed and punch him so hard in the face that my fist goes through it enough that it kills him instantly and pushes him back into a wall that he goes into the wall.

I put his crown on my head, took his sword out, cut his head off and carried it with me.

Chapter 17

I walk past the guards and they instantly see what I'm carrying and fall on their knees in fear. I stab both of them through the chest.

Once I get out of the castle it looks a little chaotic because guards are fighting with the civilians. The second they see me with Baron's head everyone is in a complete stupefied state.

I fly up to the air while holding the head out.

"Everyone take a look at your loved ones... this is the last time you will ever see them."

As I start hacking and slashing at everyone a sudden realization hits me like a bolt of lightning. I know why I was born in this kingdom now. I have to kill everyone to make sure they are no longer a threat to any person ever again. Even generations of people who are not even born yet. That's exactly what's going to happen.

Every single person in this kingdom is killed by me. While killing them I throw torches randomly in houses and all over the place too just burn this whole damn place to finally burn this place to the ground.

Once all of them were killed I fly away and make my way to Marshville. The closest kingdom to Sodom. As I flew away I couldn't help but feel contempt. I will never come back to this kingdom ever again and I've completely given up on it.

When I arrive in Marshville everything looks pretty much the same. The only difference is the fact that the place looks a lot more alive. There are people all over the place.

The second I land on the ground and purposely make the landing sound impactful every stares at me. Then suddenly drop everything, look at me completely dumb founded, and furthermore, everyone bows to me.

I fly to the main castle of the kingdom. I burst through the door.

Everyone sees me and all the guards arm themselves. Including the king. However, not with a weapon, but with the ability to light his hands on fire.

"I didn't know whether or not to believe you were dead."

"Well here is your confirmation. Either help me or get out of my way!"

The flames out of the king's hand goes away and then makes a gesture for everyone to stand down. This king has a darker skin tone and looks to be about average height. He was only five foot ten. His eyes are actually orange.

"I'm Cyrus. I'm the current king of Marshville. We've been waiting for you actually. Ever since you've come back from the dead we've been preparing to go back to war with you and take your crown back in this kingdom..."

I snapped right back, "I DON'T WANT IT BACK! I just want to make sure that there will be no people to stand in our way ever again. All I want to know is what the hell happened? Secondly, when can you get all your troops ready?"

Cyrus sits back down. "Tell the troops to prepare for war. Right after you died all of Kamar's troops came and took over everything. Within forty-eight hours. They were led by his son, Malik. After taking over the kingdom they were on the look for any super powered children. They killed all of them except me. The reason is I was the only one who was able to keep my powers a secret. Everyone else couldn't because the powers were very transparent. For example, one of them was a sixteen year old girl who had the physique of thirty years old. With very large muscles because she had superhuman strength. My powers I can keep a secret because I can summon them at will. Therefore, I can turn them off and on whenever I want. Marshville died of old age just looking after the kingdom and your children until she died. She always stayed loyal to you. She never went to anyone else. No one else ever took the throne for themselves because they knew they could not compete with you."

Eventually all the troops get ready. We are all at the front gate of the kingdom about to leave. I can see Cyrus geared up and ready to fight as well.

"No. You are not coming with us. I need someone who I can trust to be royalty until I take the world back for myself. Then I'll come back here to rule this kingdom along with the rest as the one true king."

"What will happen to me?" Cyrus barks at me.

"You will rule below me. As the second king.

Cyrus clearly is upset by this. It doesn't matter to me. Not anymore. He goes along with what I say or I will him too. I don't care about the fact that he is a descendant of mine.

The next kingdom we get to is Gamelan.

We are in front of the main gate. I'm standing right in front of everyone.

"Aside from all the children and anyone who bows to me, kill the rest."

We smash right through the front gate and do exactly that.

As soon as the last soldier has just been killed everyone else who is still alive on their knees begging for mercy.

One citizen who is also clearly a politician by the way he is dressed comes up to me, "I've never lost faith that you may return my lord. Please allow me to take control of this kingdom. I promise I won't let you down."

"No. You'll clean up the mess in this kingdom. Then I'll take care of it when I return," the tone in my voice has never been more serious.

"Just like that you trust him?" A random soldier shouts at me. "No. We take a couple of days to rest. In the meantime you and I are going to have a long talk."

Over these next three long days we have talks about what to do. Not only while I take back the rest of the kingdoms, but after.

First thing's first I take all the super powered beings and train how to use their powers. Then train them to be soldiers and kings. All the while all them are to procreate and make more super powered beings. In the meantime clean up all the dead bodies by burning those all if they never even existed. Lastly the entire time I'm gone you will make sure the laws I created before are followed now, and also enforced to everyone.

The politician agrees to all of this. I have no reason not to trust him because in his personal quarters he had a shrine to me.

The next Kingdom is Evergreen.

From the front gate I know this one is going to be the most difficult one to conquer. The reason is because they were clearly waiting for me. Archers are in towers already shooting arrows at us.

Eventually we end up killing almost everyone in the kingdom besides the women, children and the king. I saved him for last. I want to ask him some questions first.

When the king is left I throw him against the throne.

"You may have lost the battle, Jonathan, but you lost the war. You will be erased from history. No one will ever even know you existed. My great grandpa, Clyde created a full proof plan to erase you. After you died he became friends with Joshua and ended up convincing him of the truth that you killed his father.

After that he ended up going mad. He even ended up killing every single person with a superhuman power, INCLUDING his own brother, but his own mother as well. As spite for hiding from him for so long. If you think this was bad you wait until you go to Solstice and see what they did to your precious Charlotte..."

That was the exact moment I cut his head off.

The next stop has got to be Eden. The original plan is to go to Solstice. However, I have a feeling that they will be just waiting for me. Therefore, I need more soldiers.

Apparently from the looks of things even though we just arrived at Eden there has been a civil war going on within this kingdom for a while. I, along with all the other soldiers, moved very cautiously.

The thing is though this battle has been over for a while. There are bodies and blood all over the place.

Where in the hell is everyone who survived?

After searching for a while we ended up finding everyone in some sort of temple.

The temple looks like it is a dedication to me. Everyone in this temple is everyone who is not fit for a fight. Whether they are injured or otherwise.

The moment I'm recognized everyone starts chanting.

"All Hail, the golden God!"

Before I could calm everyone down a bunch of people ran up to me.

A lot of them were begging me for help.

They pulled me closer to them and some were hugging me from strong angles. One woman hugs my leg so tightly as if she was stuck to it.

"Where did all the soldiers go?"

I shout this over everyone in a very desperate tone in my voice hoping that someone responds.

"They went to the kingdom of Solstice. Because of your return they were inspired to rebel against the Kamar's dynasty here and expanded that rebellion there."

"Half of you stay here and the rest follow me to Solstice. Please let go of me."

The exact moment I burst through the front gate of the kingdom everyone had their eyes on me.

There has been a war going on here for quite a while.

I knew all of the soldiers who were on my side by the cheering. The rest look horrified.

The battle is won fairly quickly. All of the soldiers from Kamar's dynasty are dead. All civilians are spared.

Once the battle is over, everyone finally takes a sigh of relief. Except me.

I look around searching for Charlotte's tomb.

Once I find it I kneel right in front of it as if I'm praying to it.

"I was told by everyone that you fought to your dying breath. That's my girl. I know the attack was planned to happen after I passed away, but I can't help it and feel guilty about the fact that I could not be here to fight alongside you when Kamar's army attacked. I'm sure you did your best and for a fact I can say that you've definitely won back the respect of your kingdom. Also, don't worry all of those bastards that killed our children and you suffered greatly. I know you may not have felt the same way about me the way I felt about you. That being said, that does not change the fact that I did care about you deeply and I'm sorry I did not do a better job at showing it. My mistake before was not being more involved. That is exactly what I'm going to do this time. I will be the king of all four kingdoms while I let Sodom rot. I will go back and forth between all kingdoms to make sure they are run how I want them to be. I promise you this. No more distractions such as having more children and wives. I'm just going to focus on making better what I have here and now. I'll always have you in my heart. Rest peacefully now, my queen. You've earned it."

From this day forward this is exactly what I'm going to do.

Moving from kingdom to kingdom trying to run everything is very stressful, but necessary. The more I do it the more I realize how stubborn I have to be about it.

No matter how much all of the citizens want me to listen to my advisors to do things in a way that can be more beneficial to everyone. However, I know that I always have to do things my way because if I don't the past will repeat itself. If someone does not listen then they are killed on the spot.

That being said, everyone does comply. Not a single person tries to oppose me or even ask questions. This makes things a lot easier, but the unfortunate thing is because it takes such a long time to travel from kingdom to kingdom I can't keep my eyes on literally everyone. I guess that's the price I have to pay for being king of the world.

As years go on, traveling back and forth becomes harder because I could not fly as fast. Not fly as further, or even fly at all. Therefore, I had to use a horse, or a group of horses to drive the cartridge.

This time when I'm on my deathbed I'm not grasping to life as much as I
can. I'm just letting things happen.

The world is again in mourning, but it feels a lot like a stage performance. They may not be grateful now, but they will eventually become so.

"I'm not sure whether or not I'm going to come back again. Either way no matter what happens I'm going to die happy because I feel at peace that I took back control and I made everyone continue to keep the peace in my image. Furthermore, I erased any possible future threats since I wiped out the entire Kamar dynasty."

PART 3

THE APOSTATES

Chapter 18

Officially it's been one thousand years since the death of The Gold Eagle. This one thousand years includes both of the lives he dedicated to protecting people. After he died the second time the world united. Even if it was very temporary.

All kingdoms did unite and work together to keep the peace. More specifically to help keep the code that was created by The Gold Eagle in the first place. Eventually all the kingdoms became separated due to the fact that they all had different ways of how they thought Johnathan would maintain his empire. Therefore, they all broke off into different sections. It's almost like there was a kingdom within a kingdom.

This is where we come in. We are The Anointed Stalkers. We make sure that no other war will ever happen again. The way we do this is by going to sections of each kingdom and making sure that no one is out of line. In particular we keep an eye on the "false gods." Or how I like to call them "the apostates." These are the liars, the cheaters and the attention seekers. Someone will claim to be The Gold Eagle reincarnated and we go to check it out for ourselves.

There are two things in particular that we take note of. The first is how believable their claim is. Either way the test that they have to undergo will be the same. That's the second part. They will stand right in front of me while I take over their body like a puppeteer. The best part about the whole situation is that they are completely conscious about the situation.

However, there is a catch to my abilities. I can only control one person at a time because I need to be completely focused on the person I'm controlling. If I'm distracted for even a second they regain control.

For example, there was a man who literally painted himself gold and claimed to be Johnathan reincarnated. Honestly, at first I kind of believed him. He was really tall, six feet and seven inches to be specific. Clear golden skin and perfectly built frame.

Unfortunately for him it started raining when he first presented himself to us. Of course, the golden that he painted on him was starting to slip off of him due to the water. He tried hiding it, but couldn't.

Just to mess with him I kept playing along for some time, but I eventually took complete control of him. I made him pick up a random axe and made him drive it into his skull.

Thankfully I was able to get him to drive an ax into his skull a split second before I was about to be hit by someone, who I assume is close to him. Any second later he would have been able to stop.

"Another false god has been executed for blasphemy!" I shout at the top of my lungs.

I along with all the other anointed ones turn around and head on our way.

My name is Nyla Howler and at the age of twenty five I'm the youngest and first female leader of The Anointed Stalkers.

We headed back to our home.

I could help but admire our team and how far we'd come since the creation of The Anointed Stalkers.

From what I've been told the history of our organization goes way back. Way before I was even born.

The Stalkers were created shortly after Johnathan's second death. After they knew for a fact he can come back to life by being reborn, a bunch of people started telling stories about it, about Johnathan and everything he did in both lifetimes.

Those stories were told for the past one thousand years. Since these stories were told over and over again and by countless different people this resulted in these stories being altered.

Altered so much that it felt like no one was telling the truth anymore. Just what they wanted everyone to hear. This is what caused the hundreds of factions being created in each kingdom. These factions generated all these false prophets.

Therefore, that's what resulted in our organization being created. Matthias Mortimer is the man who created The Anointed Stalkers.

The Purgatory's Immortals was the name of the faction he was originally part of. Their belief was that Johnathan had already returned. He has just not found the right physical form yet. In the meantime he will hop from body to body to use them as vessels to pass on a message. This message was to send all of the immortals on a mission to recruit as many followers as possible. That's because currently they are all in purgatory until Johnathan returns in his true form. Hence their name.

Matthias was born into this faction and believed in it most of his life. The problem was the more people they got to convert the more advantage they took of them. That's what resulted in Matthias figuring out that he was being taught lies.

At the age of twenty-four Matthias was told that finally Johnathan was reincarnated again. Of course everyone was absolutely ecstatic to have him return. Every one of the members of this faction met at a temple to see him. Stupidly, the imposter expected literally no one else in the world to come to see him. Besides everyone who was a part of The Immortal's Purgatory faction.

Therefore, he was extremely concerned when he was shaking hands with everyone who was an outsider. Eventually someone decided to stab him in the center of the chest to test him. He instantly goes from being praised to being booed. Everyone starts to spit on him and hit while he is bleeding to death.

In that exact moment Matthias walked away from everything. While everyone else was screaming and yelling that they were lied to he just walked away. The reason is because he was so broken-hearted that he had no idea what to do next.

For weeks he aimlessly wandered around the world. The depression just caved in for him. He would purposely not eat or take care of himself in any way. If anyone even offered him help in any way he would turn it down. As a matter of fact he would act very aggressive and rude towards these people. To the point where they thought he was dangerous. Therefore, they all stayed away from him.

Everything changed when he had a life altering dream.

Matthias was standing and wandering in a skeleton graveyard that is also covered in fog. From the fog a gold covered man emerges. The golden man looks like he is sixty feet tall.

He sees him and starts moving towards him. Matthias tries to run away as quickly as he can and of course he does not get away because his reach is too long. He picks him up and brings him really close to his face. He has this look on his face as if he is dead inside.

"I'm disappointed, Matthias. All I wanted from you is to help prepare as many people as possible for my return. Instead you sat back and did nothing. Therefore you must be punished."

The golden man's voice sounds otherworldly. As if every word that he says echoes and vibrates. The sounds those words make automatically demand authority. Even though he is holy talking to one person, these are words that are meant to be heard by everyone.

Then the gold man moves Matthias towards his mouth as if he is about to eat him.

At that moment Matthias woke up from his dream sweaty and restless. However, he also woke up with a purpose.

For the next several weeks he dedicated his time to making himself better in all aspects of his life. The first part, of course, was the physical aspect of his life. Eating properly again, getting all his strength back and even started to exercise.

The second part was his mental wellbeing. More specifically his mentality improved a lot due to all the education that he soaked up. During this time period of self-restoration, Matthias took advantage of the kindness of others.

He uses their kindness to study the different factions and sees how they operate. He takes notice of a lot of the exact same beliefs that everyone does.

Yes, there are the only obvious common aspects. Such as all of us unanimously believe that only a superhero actually existed at one point in time, but one day he will return to save us all once again from all the evil of this world. On top of that all factions agree that we are all here to contribute. No one is here to deliberately bring harm to anyone. However, the most important recurring variable is the fact that we are all supposed to continue living the same way he taught us while Johnathan was alive.

That's when Matthias had a giant revelation. He needs to start telling people new ideas about Johnathan. Not in the sense that he has to make stuff up. More in the sense that he has given people a new message that will give them more hope than any other faction has given before.

The message of hope was, "we don't have to continue following the rules that Johnathan established. If he returned before he'll return again. Therefore, we have to prepare for that because then he will give new rules to follow."

Surprisingly this new message worked. People started to listen to it. However, that being said it did not last very long with people. The main reason was because he did come up with some kind of plan for it.

Within the span of a month almost all of the followers that Matthias got he lost.

Everything changed when he noticed that there were a lot of apostates showing up in these factions. The lie that Johnathan has been reincarnated and is back helping people. This is what led to creating the rule for us to kill all apostates.

No one really knows the exact reason as to why Matthias resorted to killing. This is one of the few aspects of the history of our faction that is very inconsistent. However, I personally think it is entirely due to jealous rage. Simply because of the fact he felt like he was chosen by Johnathan himself to save people and the fact that he was failing at it resulted in him killing people to take out his anger on people. To me that just seems logical. Nevertheless this was the choice that solidified us as a faction that actually had an impact on the world.

After killing one apostate he kept going. This is how he got more people to join us. A lot of people had their eyes open and it was a breath of fresh air for people to have someone who did not teach them lies.

That being said, a lot of the first generation of The Anointed Stalkers did not really agree with our message. They were just using this filter of, "we are creating a new world for The Golden Phoenix to return" as an excuse to indulge in their bad behavior. Matthias never complained about this because he felt like the goal that needed to be achieved was being achieved.

Once the second generation of The Anointed Stalkers came into the picture then things started to take shape.

The first impactful thing that we did was just simply existing longer than any other faction. Every other faction by that point would fall apart or start to. The reason is because either they start to fight against each other or someone was able to disprove their entire belief system. That's why we were able to get more followers as time went on.

The second and most important part was that we actually were able to start building our own kingdom. Luna Wane, who was the daughter of Matthias, had become his successor. She was born with supernatural abilities therefore, she had an inherited bias towards them. That resulted in her focusing more on getting super powered followers, not just normal ones. That being said, all the ones that did not have super powers were still used to help achieve this goal. Everyone who was not super powered just helped build our kingdom and make sure everything was run properly. We built the kingdom in the center of the world because we felt like we were the ones bringing balance to it. Those who had powers were constructed into an army to go after the protesters in particular.

Luna had the ability to change her arms into any weapon she desired. Therefore, that is why whenever she went after other apostates and killed them a lot more resistance was in her way. She either always had the right tool to use or people were just so afraid of her to stand up to her.

As the years went on Luna realized that there was a fear that would constantly hit her like a punch to the gut. What if we run out of super powered people to convert? Even though we had a literal super powered army it was a small one. No more than fifty people.

That's what began our "breeding cycle." Basically everyone who had a super power were the only people allowed to have kids. Everyone else was not. The majority of the mothers did not have super powers. This was done on purpose so that way they had less risk of being in danger. Whenever a super powered woman was pregnant she was kept in the kingdom as well for the same reason.

These ideas of our faith were kept the same for centuries. Eventually our kingdom was done being built and we decided to give it the name of The Chosen Pioneers. We are just preparing a new world for Johnathan to explore and we were chosen to be by his side. Now that being said I think after this is when we started to become selfish.

I'm not trying to change our rules, it's just contradicting. I understand that we are trying to prepare the world for his return, but to me it does not make sense why that means we sit back and let everything else just rot away. We are told to never interfere in people's lives because that's not our job. That's what Johnathan's going to do. So, then why do we kill all the apostates? Isn't that interfering?

This is very similar to what happened in The Peacemonger Faction. That is where I was originally from before I came here. It is located in a more eastern Asian part of the world.

The Peacemonger Faction believed that we are here to help people and only that. If we do anything we are not following the faction's rules. As a matter of fact they would kick you out if you broke this rule. That is exactly what happened to me. I was born and raised in this faction. I was so on top of following their rules that I felt like I knew them better than the rest. That of course meant that I stood up to people and lost my temper on others when I felt like they did not understand our rules. This is what got me kicked out. Peacemongers believe that they are here to only help to such an extreme that it's the only thing they will do. If anyone causes any kind of harmful gesture in any way you're kicked out. Even if you stand up to someone for bullying anyone else, for example. This is seen as harmful behavior because I caused them harm by not letting the bully help their victim "in their own way." That's what we were constantly told. "Everyone has their own way of helping, therefore we must interfere and just trust in what they are doing." To me that was total bullshit.

Once I was officially kicked out I was homeless for what seemed like an eternity. Even though it was a horrible experience I hope to never go through again there were some really good things that came out of this experience.

The first obviously is that I came across The Anointed Stalkers. More specifically to be honest I should say they came across me.

I was in a more eastern Asian part of the world when I first got kicked out. Therefore, there were a lot of close-by factions for me to seek aid from. However, that never happened. The reason is The Peacemongers had a reputation of shunning every other faction besides their own. Simply because they had a different view on violence. So, whenever someone would figure out that I was part of their faction they would shun me.

I guess what goes around comes around.

The Anointed Stalkers eventually found me in a faction called The Sect of Kinship. This was the only faction that welcomed me with open arms without judging me in any way.

They are a faction focused much more on the "pleasure-able" side of life. They believed that since Johnathan had countless children which resulted in him having countless descendants they felt like they had to continue doing that so he does not get wiped out of history.

Pleasure is the main objective of this entire faction. Therefore, what could be done to achieve that sensation? Whether it is getting crazy drunk, having sex until you pass out from exhaustion, or any other way pleasure can be felt.

Ironically though the more I dived into the void of pleasure the more empty I felt. To fix this empty feeling I looked for a way to help people. I couldn't help myself. I had to find a way to do that in any way I can.

I only focused on finding a way to help this faction and everyone in it. Nothing else.

The first thing I thought of doing to give more pleasure to this faction is by creating many different types of wines for people to drink. They were all flavors that they never tasted before, they were all a lot stronger too. Furthermore, I just tried to help people in any way I could.

Helping spread the word of parties.

Helping people get with other people they specifically have a crush on.

I actually helped people so much more than I realized that people started to look up to me as if I was some sort of leader. Even though I never wanted to be one. I was just trying to help.

People of course started to get jealous that I was being seen as a leader. More than anything they felt like I was promoting a false agenda because this faction never had a leader before. I always debunked these claims, but a lot of people would not believe me.

It was around this same time that I found out I had the ability to control people.

One of the residents who started looking up to me as a leader one day tried to seduce me. I tried my best to turn her down. The problem was that she did not get the message.

She actually tried over and over to come onto me. Eventually her husband finds out he kills her out of rage and tries to kill me after words.

One day when she tries to seduce me her husband follows her. He sees her trying to be seductive and kills her by stabbing her to death then tries to kill me the same way.

However, suddenly when I fell back in fear and held my hand up he couldn't move. He clearly could still see what he was doing. I then told him to stab himself in the neck and kill himself. He tried to fight it as hard as he could, but nothing happened.

The screaming obviously caught the attention of all the towns folk. I was totally up front with everyone and after they were buried and everything was settled no more than a week later The Anointed Stalkers showed up.

I was told by them that they were told to come here because of me. I never knew who ratted me out, but when they did their investigation they did not want to kill me, but collaborate with me.

It was because like them I did not want to tell them a false story that I was Johnathan reincarnated that I just tried to help like he was.

That's how I became one of their followers.

Chapter 19

Of course this does not mean they welcomed me with open arms. I had to prove myself. There were countless trials for me to pass and I had to earn their trust. While I was with them this feeling of wanting to help others never left me.

My power was the thing that they gave the most attention to. I was very willing to listen to them to do the best I can to push that power to the limit because I didn't know what I could do at my full potential either.

What I realized at the end was that what I could do mentally all depended on how much physically I was willing to push myself. If I really wanted to, I could probably control five people at a time or even more. However, I'm afraid of making my head explode or something.

The next set of skills I had to learn I already knew. Those skills are learning how to fight and protect myself. Not just with my fists, but swords, spears, and every other weapon imaginable. That's not because I was better than anyone or that it was easier for me to learn. I just knew how to do it. Not sure how to describe it really. It's just one of those instinctual feelings that people get. I just know this is how each weapon is used.

The final test was to see if I was willing to kill the people who are running Johnathan's image. That was never a problem to me. I always looked up to Johnathan and because he was willing to kill to save the world, I will do the same to live up to his name.

I rose up through the ranks fairly quickly because everything they told me to do I did it. To the exact detail that order was given to me I listened. Within no more than three years I became the runner up to be leader of The Anointed Stalkers.

The day I became the leader of this faction is a day I will never forget. Not just because of that, but also it is the day I figured out I had a second superpower I never knew I had. Unbreakable skin.

A new faction started to get some attention for claiming that they are following the rules of both Johnathan and his twin brother, Kamar. They called themselves The Twin's Heirs.

That was already a red flag for me because over a thousand years' worth of history was written about Johnathan and never once did it ever mention a brother. If it was up to me I would have killed them all for spreading this lie. However, at the time I was not the leader so I could not make that decision.

Nevertheless, at first they were left alone because they did not have any apostates in their faction, just different beliefs. The problems started to crop up when they were spreading the word that they are changing the world in the way the twins wanted them too.

We did not know the exact details at the time, but basically, similar to us, they wanted to shape the world for Johnathan's return. The difference was that they decided who deserved to see this "new" world.

Mara Brock is the leader of The Twins' Heirs faction.

At first when we went there everything was calm and everyone got along. We got invited to have dinner with them at this long table where you could fit like one hundred people.

Then Mara had to start talking. "Its amazing how two brothers could have shared the same partner? I've never heard of that before."

Or.

"They were so close that whenever anyone was rude to either of them they would be instantly punished."

I don't know what exactly, but whenever this bitch let a word out of her mouth with anything to do with Johnathan I wanted to kill her. It's like she was saying something personal to me. As if she was trying to attack me personally. I wanted to slit her throat. Therefore, I did.

Really I should say, I tried to.

She had the ability to move superfast.

Without even realizing it, Mara moved so fast that she grabbed the sword in my hand to attack and stabbed our leader, Augustus Lament instead.

"Eye for an eye." Mara shouts as she moves away from the table with all of her followers.

The thing that I took note of though was the fact that she moved at a more average pace now. Also, she looked a little out of breath.

It appears to me that even though she has superhuman speed, it only lasts as long as many calories she takes in. Therefore, I took my shot.

I pulled out my second sword and went after her. I thought some of the others were going to come with me, but they all stayed back to fight her followers. However, looking back on this moment, it's probably because they were hoping I'd end up dead.

A bunch of people were in my way. I killed them all. Whether it was by sword or by the fact that I used my mind controlling abilities. Although that was a lot harder because I could not focus on my targets as much.

Eventually I got through them all and I managed to find a door that was barricaded with things in front of it and a bunch of guards. Five guards to be specific.

The biggest guy was over seven feet tall and huge. He literally looked like a man sized bear. I knew I could not fight him, in particular he is like twice my height and three times my size. All I could do is just focus as much of my energy as possible to control him.

Thankfully it worked, but I felt like my head was going to explode from the pain because he is such a big man. My nose started to bleed a bit from the pain.

After I got him to kill the rest of the guards and used him to break the door then grab a knife to stab himself in the eye.

I walk into the room and Mara is all by herself and she is just eating like crazy. Every possible food you can think of is in this room. It's like an all you eat buffet.

She looks a little shocked because of the door being broken. She looked calm and confident.

I remember in that exact moment, in my gut I had a feeling I was about to die. However, I had to keep fighting, to try, to keep going.

Thankfully I didn't die. She again moved so fast I could not see her with a sword in her hand.

However, when she stopped moving not only was she out of breath, but the sword looked like it was beaten down to the handle.

Mara shouts at me, "How is this possible? I stabbed you like fifty times and not a single cut on your body!"

I smirk at her and cut her head clean off. I spit on her corpse right after.

As soon as Mera's people realized she was killed some of them wanted to join us. I declined and left them all here.

We all go back home and take Augutus' corpse with us.

When we arrive everyone is instantly in tears that our leader is gone.

We instantly prepare a ceremony to bury him. However, instantly after we did the ceremony that made me the next leader. Even though I did not want to do the ceremony right away I thought it would be better to wait. To let people grieve and recover from this tragedy, but they insisted so I listened.

I kept all the traditions of the faction and tried my best to be the leader people needed.

It worked. That's because we managed to keep balance in the world. We kill all the apostates who have our little empire built, everyone here is happy and everyone is doing the best with what they have.

Our faction is blossoming and it's like we've built a brand new kingdom. People who live here are prospering. Buildings are built on a strong foundation that will last for centuries. It's so well put together here that you would not be able to know all the troubles that everyone else has out there.

Compared to every other family that has a house with holes in the roof and ripped furniture, we have built homes that are brand new, cleaned and filled with everything that a family would need in it.

And yet still people don't trust me. They don't have faith in me. They still think that I got Augustus killed out of my own selfish goals. Even though there are a bunch of witnesses to tell them otherwise.

Nonetheless I still got to try to help as many people as possible and in this kingdom and everyone else as much as I can without breaking any rules.

This is done by me through the use of new "followers" to our faction. Every once in a while we have new people coming to this faction because it has "better living conditions." Instead of accepting them and worrying about overpopulation I would turn them down. In secret, without them even knowing, as they turned around to go back home I would give them a tool that they would need to fix their faction. It was not some kind of magical tool, but it was a tool that is the root to helping fix a problem. For example, a family came here because they wanted to feel more of a sense of protection because they have no means to protect themselves. I put weapons into their carriage in secret and they have those weapons now.

A smile grows on my face whenever I give a tool back to someone. I know this does not guarantee that I help them or that I fix their problem, but I feel like I did my part while respecting the rules of our faction.

Thankfully it was working to the point where we've been having an impact on the other factions. Therefore, there are less apostates and more cooperation. Which means that the other factions started to listen to the rules we applied to our faction.

Things are finally calming down and people's blame towards me slowly dissolves. However, suddenly another apostate starts to present himself to the world. The most notable thing about this one is the fact that he actually had unbreakable skin and some people are starting to actually believe he is the reincarnated version of Jonathan.

It's terrifying to hear that.

The reason is because whenever someone with unbreakable skin is discovered they are automatically labeled an apostate and therefore are killed. That's why I can never tell them about my secret power.

People with unbreakable skin are automatically labeled apostates because they are threats. Ever since Johnathan's second death there has been this bullseye that has been put on him by everyone. Not just to avoid a third world war, but the fact that he had such a chaotic personality which led to a bunch of more problems. Therefore, even though everyone always hopes that he can come back no one actually wants him too.

Which I never thought made sense to me, but I never really complained about it because when he actually does come back no one will be able to contain him anyway.

That's beside the point that I don't think we should be killing someone who has not done anything wrong. I'm trying my best to convince them not to do it and not only are they not agreeing with me, they actually despise me for it.

"I'm being a bad example," is what everyone is saying.

"Tough shit!" That's my response to that. "It's not because I'm the leader. It's because it's not right. We can't go around killing people that have done nothing. On top of that this person is not acting like a false prophet. SO DROP IT!"

I continued to shout at everyone.

"Johnathan would not go around just killing people just because they might be a problem. He only stepped in when he needed to. When there was a problem."

One of the other members of The Anointed Stalkers shouts back to me, "How the fuck do you know?"

"I just do, all right? I studied him for a long time and I felt like I actually understood him."

All of them looked right at me in complete frustration and as if they wanted to kill me. They all just leave the room aggressively and just leave me alone abandoned in this room.

It's late in the night so I'm just going to go to sleep.

Suddenly in the middle of the night I hear chanting. I can't quite make out what it is. However, I go closer to the window to see what it is.

It is the entire kingdom chanting, "FALSE GOD," at me while holding torches and weapons moving towards me. At the front of this chanting mob there are two of the anointed stalkers with the dead body of a man.

There are no scratches on him... wait! Is that the unbreakable man? They somehow found a way to kill him?

I got to get out of here.

My first instinctual feeling is to try to talk everyone down, but their mind is made up. Second of all, if they find a way to kill one person with unbreakable skin, how long until they find a way to kill me. Therefore, I must leave.

I waste no time and go out the back window. I just got right out of it. I landed right on the ground with no problems or injuries because of the unbreakable skin.

At this exact moment no other word or action was echoing more through my mind then, RUN!

Chapter 20

As I stare at the bright and orange fire, while I try to keep warm I can't help but feel like a failure.

Taking another aggressive bite of the deer that I cooked for myself and I don't know what my next move is going to be.

No other faction is going to welcome me in because everyone knows who I am and everyone will have a vendetta against me. On top of that, if I decide to dedicate the rest of my life to helping others I will be painting even a bigger target on my back because everyone will think I'm trying to be the next Golden Phoenix. Therefore, The Anointed Stalkers will be after me.

What the fuck do I do?

Wait! I got it.

What if I'm not the one who does all the heroic acts?

What if I just give the other heroes their direction?

How to do things? What to do and so on. Yes, that's perfect. Where do I begin?

I can't start my own faction because that will automatically raise the eyebrows of everyone. Maybe I can start by becoming a lone vigilante. Not for forever though. Just long enough to have an impact. To inspire people to do the same thing. Then I will stop and just live my life normally. If no one wants me to be a part of their faction because I interfere too with their rules so be it. I'll just be alone forever. Then I won't be a bother to anyone anymore.

It's not that I'm letting people's opinion of me affect my own selfimage, but that's the only way I can give back to the people while still respecting the rules that were established and keeping myself safe.

All right so how do I start approaching this goal? Well, firstly I have to think what kind of hero do I want to be? More specifically, what kind of hero do I want to aspire people to be?

I want to emulate what Johnathan did. However, I feel like that will give the wrong message to people. Even though he has killed a bunch of people while he was alive I can't do the same thing. I need to give people a more positive message. A more optimistic one. I feel like if I do what he did I could promote a pessimistic message. Therefore, the number one rule I have to always keep in mind is: no killing. I want people to think that heroes are here to help. To do well. Not bring harm to any person whatsoever. Even if it is someone who is a bad person committing a crime.

The second rule is to never over step people's boundaries. This means that all I do is just a heroic act and nothing else. I never escalate things to the point where I tell people how to act or take charge and force them to follow my lead. They must choose for themselves whether or not to become heroes. If I force them to follow, this can cause the creation of another faction which I don't want.

As the sun rises and shines right into my eyes the idea of the costume enters my brain. I will of course wear a mask because I already have a target on my back, but the costume itself will make me look like a bumble bee.

A yellow costume with black lines on it which will put an emphasis on the main parts of my body. Such as my abs and chest for instance. It will be a costume that will be an homage to his, but stand on its own.

Now I have to get the materials. I know where to get them, but how do I get them?

As I start to head towards the faction of Gangland a bunch of different ways of how I can get the suit. I don't have any money and I can't make the costume myself. I've never learned how to sew. At the same time I don't want to do anything illegal. Maybe working for them will help.

Arriving in Gangland feels like a complete culture shock to me. Even though I read all about this faction throughout the years it was still surreal how crazy this place is.

The way this faction works is like a game of rock, paper, and scissors. One gang keeps going up against another until it wins. Once it wins another does the same thing. You keep repeating the same thing over and over again until the end of time. That's what all the research I've done about them says while I was doing my studies.

Therefore, that's why not many people live here and a lot have fled. It is not a safe place to be in at all. That's why my guard is always up as if I'm about to be in another fight.

They never expanded outside of their faction because of how big an impact The Anointed Stalkers had.

I get to a store called, "The Cloth King." The owner is not around at the moment so as I am waiting for him I look around. These costumes are beautiful. The colors, the patterns, the attention to detail. They look like military uniforms.

"What kind of costume do you want?"

A voice asks behind me. As I turned around I saw a very tall but skinny man. He is well into his sixties, however he looks great for his age.

"How much do you want for it?" I ask cautiously.

"Don't worry about it." He says calmly.

My eyebrows jump up.

"What do you mean? With all due respect, that sounds a little suspicious to me."

The owner sighs, "I never get any money from any costume I make. The reason is because my payment is protection and safety from everyone in the faction. No one is allowed to hurt me and if something happens to me whether I get sick or otherwise everyone immediately comes to my aid. I'm the top priority of this faction. That's my reward for creating the costumes."

I'm honestly speechless. Thankfully this all happened very conveniently to me. Or really anyone that does not have any money.

"A sun yellow costume with parts of it being black that highlights certain parts of my body! Also, a mask that covers my entire face besides my eyes."

He nods and immediately starts working.

As he is making the costume, taking my measurements, seeing which variant of yellow and black works, he puts certain pieces of it on me to see how it fits.

The moment he starts doing that flashes of moments appear in my head. For example, when he puts on the arm piece a flash of a piece of armor coming through my skin.

What are these moments?

The moments keep popping up in my head. With each piece of the costume being put on me. When he finally finished the full costume, I put the mask on. This triggered something really badly in me because I started to hyperventilate and shake uncontrollably. I run immediately out of the store and hide somewhere that is completely abandoned.

Are these permissions? Is Johnathan reaching out to me from the dead? Either way it does not matter. This must mean something, but what? I can't think about that too much. I have to stay focused on my goal.

After the suit is fully on me for the first time I take a good look. I could not help, but feel a giddy sensation in my gut. However, more moments in my brain started to flash before my eyes.

This moment is of a moment where an entire shit comes from underneath my skin and when I look in front of me there is someone with a knife trying to attack me.

What is happening to me?

I slapped myself in the face a few times. STOP GETTING DISTRACTED GODDAMMIT!

Focus! All right so... you are in a faction called Gangland. How do you help people here? Well, by stopping the violence. However, the only way to do that is taking the things away that contribute to the violence. It may not stop it but calm it down. Therefore, I must destroy all weapons. I need to also create a sign that tells everyone that this hero I'm trying to be is inspired by "The Golden God."

I'm sure I'll find a way, but right now I need to find a way to get rid of those weapons.

Which gang should I get rid of their weapons first? Not the gang who has the title currently because if I do that I will take every means of defending themselves. Their weapons should be destroyed last. All right so I need to destroy each gang from most problematic to least problematic then I slowly inspire people along the way and when they decide to become heroes themselves I will leave to the next faction. I can't stay here forever, because the heroes who are inspired by me need to think for themselves too.

I sneak into a random gang's headquarters. There are random guards still guarding a random shack at this headquarters. I command them both to enter it to see if the weapons are there. Luckily there are also fireworks in this shack as well. One guard puts the weapons in one pile. The other sets up the fireworks. I needed to be very careful which fireworks I told him set off because I don't want to send the wrong message. I pick the fireworks that will show the image of a phoenix with a sword and shield around it. The other guard takes a lantern and smashers it against the weapons. And the other aims the fireworks right next to the fire. Thankfully I was able to control both enough to also keep their mouth shut. However, contorting two people at the same time gave me such a bad headache it made me pass out just as the fireworks went up into the air and made the shape of exactly what I wanted when they went off. Also, the guards ran away and I passed out in a stack of hay.

When I wake I finally have some energy back. However, I still need fuel to get the rest of it back. Where is the nearest water fountain and plate of food? Thankfully, there is a water fountain a few feet away from me. I pull the rope that has a bucket attached to it and drink the water right out of the bucket without thinking.

Now where do I find food? The barn where all the animals are. Often farmers leave food for the animals so I'll look there. Yes, the food might be old and maybe moldy, but it won't affect me due to the unbreakable skin. Most importantly it's fuel for my body.

I eventually get to a barn that is filled with animals. There is a bunch of food on the ground and thankfully it does not look that old. I pushed the animals out of the way and ate as much as I could. Eventually I stopped eating because the bad taste took over my hunger.

Back to the mission!

Unfortunately my first fireworks show did not really have much of an impact. It's not that I expected everyone to instantly become superheroes and dedicate their lives to saving people, but it's like nothing even happened in the first place.

Therefore, what I'm going to do from now on is make fireworks at every crime I stop. If there are not any there I will use whatever I can around me to make a symbol that gives people the impression that the act was inspired by The Golden Guardian. I just hope that it actually inspires people enough to become heroes.

The next crime I stop is random mugging. There are no fireworks anywhere so I tell the person I saved to spread the word that my actions were inspired by The Golden Guardian and that she should spread the word about it.

With this and the constant symbols that I leave after every crime I stop momentum starts to build. Gangs start to break apart and the super powered people start to go their own way. This also slows the crime rate a bit because all of this happens for one gang to announce to the others that they are trying to take over the faction. Therefore, people step in to try and stop it before it even happens. They all may not have decided to become vigilantes, but they are helping people with the powers they have. This may result in things becoming more chaotic. However, this is not my problem because that's out of my control and I'm just here to inspire people to go their own way. Also, I was able to keep my identity a secret while helping all these people because of the costume. Everyone is looking for, what they assume is a man in a golden and black costume. That's why whenever I take it off I just go about my day as if I have nothing to worry about.

After I save someone from having their house broken into this is the only time I have to ask for something else besides spreading the word. I ask them for help and thankfully they agree. I save it all for tonight and tomorrow because I will be heading to the next faction to do the exact same thing.

However, I can't go to some random faction. I have to go to the Star Chasers. This faction is preparing for signs from the universe that Johnathan is returning. In the meantime they are preparing as many weapons as possible so that when these signs are seen they will start to create his one world unity again.

These signs are as follows:

1. There will literally be a sign in the sky signaling that he will return soon. This signal in particular will be of literal announcement that he is returning.
2. Divine power will take control of the Star Chasers.
3. Lastly, every other faction will no longer follow a false narrative about The Golden Guardian and start following the appropriate one.

When reading about this faction in my studies I felt like they were one of the few that were actually crazy. Their hypocrisy is bizarre to me. They wait for signals for Johnathan to return, but they need to prepare certain things for him to return. As one example. Once he does return they want to kill him to not start another war, and they will continue the world in his image how they saw it.

Learning about all the factions felt like something I needed to do. Ever since I decided to take my faith super seriously back home. If I wanted to become the best I needed to learn about the rest. Or else I would not know the difference between knowing how to follow in Johnathan's footsteps properly or not.

What I'm going to do is take advantage of their rules and use them in my favor. This will hopefully get the message world wide a lot quicker that things are changing. Hopefully, their looney behavior will spread that message quicker because everyone will know that my mission was influenced by Johnathan. Therefore, feel compelled to follow or.

While I start to put this plan into action a dark thought enters my mind: no matter how successful this mission is, I will never have a calm life ever again. Even if I manage to keep my unbreakable skin a secret I will always have The Anointed Stalkers coming after me. My mission will be successful in time and they will know that I started it. At first I was hoping that the tower burning was going to be convincing enough for them to believe that I died. However, if there is no body that would be naïve of them. Therefore, while I accomplish this mission I need to prepare myself for some sort of a final stand between me and them. Whether it is physical or otherwise.

Having picked out a bunch of fireworks in a bag I am able to set them up in a way that when they go off they will leave a message in the sky. I know this because on the side of each firework is a label describing what it shows when it goes off.

I need to choose a proper message for the fireworks to make. The fireworks can't just say something simple like, "I'm coming soon." It just seems too good to be true and I don't think this faction will take it seriously. While I think about that I need to try to test my mind control powers more. Before this point I've never felt like I had to use them for my own benefit. More importantly because I never wanted to use those powers for my own benefit. However, this is an exception. Yes, in the previous faction I used my powers to control two adults, but how does it affect children? Or even animals? That's what I need to figure out.

It seems to be very similar to humans. It depends how difficult each brain is to control. If some animals have smaller brains than others the more I can control. Not just one but even a group of animals. A group of cats can be very simple to control and so can dogs, but dogs are slightly more difficult. To compare and contrast they if I can mind control five average size cats then three medium size dogs.

While testing out my powers I once again look for food in the garbage. I found some but not as much. I still eat it and this one looks older. After I eat it I start to feel a bit sick. However, it can't be from food because that has never affected me before, it must be from me testing my power.

I have to maintain my secrecy while being in this faction because if they see me and then all these bizarre things will happen they won't believe them to be real. They will think they are illusions made by people to manipulate the town to follow a ruler. I know this because a long time ago some did try to falsely pass the message that he is here. They ended up publicly executing this person to teach everyone in this town in a lesson. Not for spreading lies, but what they will do when Johnathan actually returns. Conditioning people so much so that every action they will make at that point will be done by instinct.

"Take arms and prepare yourselves. Heroes will rise again."

That is the message I send out through the fireworks at exactly midnight. I'm not sure how everyone will respond to it, but I need to hide so no one suspects me.

I end up coming across a barn and hiding in there. It is filled with so many animals that it feels like there is no space to walk around. Therefore I end up going to the second level of it via a ladder to be separated from them and then hopefully remain hidden until I know what the response to that message will be. Even if I wanted to sleep I can't because the smells are so bad.

Fuck me I think I'm going to puke. I've been feeling kind of sick all day. I'm trying my best to hold it in, but the smell is exculpating that feeling and it is starting to give me a headache. This is really strange to me because due to the unbreakable skin I should be invulnerable, no?

That does not matter because I end up puking and so much so that I end up passing out.

"WAKE UP!"

This instantly wakes me up. I see an older man standing over me looking very confused.

"Oh thank goodness you found me instead of some monster. When I saw the message in the clouds I ran away in fear because I thought it meant that it was the end of the world. I packed a bag and ran. I started to get tired so I decided to take shelter here. My apologies sir I can leave now if you'd like."

I'm clearly putting a show on for him.

"Go? Where do you go? You have to come to the temple with us to be spiritually prepared since the first sign has been shown. Get ready because we are leaving soon."

"Yes. Of course how foolish of me to forget."

Before we all went to the temple this nice man gave me a new charge of clothes, food, and a place where I can clean myself up. While doing all of these things I spark a conversation with him getting to know him and this faction more.

Firstly, this man's name is Juan.

The second thing he explained to me was that we all go to the temple to meditate and wait for the second sign. We all have to wait at the temple because that is where all of the weapons as well. Ironic, but whatever. Anyway, if the second sign does present itself to the people then they have to take up arms to start their revolution. That's because this will be the third signal. Once this revolution is over, everyone will no longer follow false narratives.

While we are heading to the temple I'm trying to think I can convince everyone that the signal is presenting itself to everyone.

I also notice that everyone seems forced to go to this temple whether they want to or not. Children in particular make this point clear to me by the attitude they show their parents. Wait a minute does this mean that even children are part of their revolution?

Arriving at the temple the beautiful architecture of it just completely puts me in a state of awe. This is a huge temple that is at least fifty feet in height. The handles of the doors are designed to look like wings. All the windows on the outside have a unique color to them. This color compliments whatever picture the window has in it. For example, one window is colored green. This window has a picture of The Phoenix standing in front of a throne that he wants to take for him.

Inside of the temple the beauty continues to have an effect on me. This clearly is the most important building in the entire faction. It has the most care, money and presentation given to it.

We all sit on the benches and just wait. Then all of sudden a giant door with a group of people just opens from the back. Each person has a weapon on their hand. Behind them is a bunch of other weapons. It's like a shack filled with weapons. You could give one weapon to an entire army and you'd still have thousands left.

This group of people start motioning their hands as if they are encouraging others to come and pick up weapons too. Even the children.

Instantly I try to control the children to stop. I am not able to stop them all at once but I was able to stop three. These children lose the group of their parents and run out of the temple.

"WHAT THE HELL DO YOU THINK YOU ARE DOING?" One parent shouts this so loudly that it makes everyone's toes curl in their shoes.

This shouting made me lose my concentration.

The kid runs back to his father crying.

"DADDY IT WAS NOT ME! I was forced to run away."

The father clearly does not believe him.

The other two kids say in unison. "Me too."

Everyone suddenly gasps and falls to their knees.

I GOT THEM!

I'll take the control of one of the group members and force them to throw a couple of candles on the weapons and burn them all. This results in everyone else who had a weapon to throw them on top of the burning pile as well.

I know taking their weapons is only going to be a delay in terms of how much excessive violence they will bring to the other factions. However, I need to protect as many lives as I can in the meantime.

As we all walk out of the temple we march toward the next faction like an army. I'm in the back of the army which is fine by me because that means less people will take notice of me when I change into my costume.

I can't just rely on the hope that people will start to become vigilantes to protect their people from The Star Chasers invasion. Therefore, secretly as they start to spread their message to the people I will protect those who come in harm's way and therefore that leads to the desire for that domino effect to start.

Chapter 21

As The Star Chasers start wiping out other factions I stay in the costume in the background of all the battles.

I unfortunately can't save every innocent person who gets caught in the crossfire, but this is the only way. Whether I was here or not when The Guardian came back there is going to be another war anyway. It is inevitable. No matter how badly everyone wants to avoid it.

While I save people others do the same and fight back. This does not guarantee that this act or heroism will lead more. However, it is the start.

Star Chasers go from faction to faction wiping out as many people as possible. Ironically though in the meantime the third sign presents itself. That's because I leave wing symbols on doors, windows and so on. Therefore, more people decide to join because this proves The Star Chaser's point that they are given divine signs that he is coming back soon. However, it is clear to me that some are just joining just hoping to be spared.

This crusade goes on for countless hours. I can't even tell the next time anyone got a proper night's rest or even a belly full of food.

When it is pitch black outside I stayed a bit behind in the faction that was just demolished so I can't change back into regular clothes. Thankfully no one saw me.

What's concerning to me is that it is only a matter of time before The Anointed Stalkers find out where The Chasers are. Therefore, we have to kill them before they get to us and find out I'm still alive. The thing is though the Chasers are nervous to attack them because of a fear of losing.

I need to find a way to send a message to the rest of them that they should be the next target and in particular that they need to have faith that they will win that battle. How do I do that? It is pitch black outside and I know my powers can't force people to speak for me. Furthermore, there are thousands of us in the army and how can I send a message that everyone can see and not suspect me of doing it. Lastly, I don't have any fireworks left with me so I have to figure out an alternative method to communicate with everyone.

The thing is though if all The Anointed Stalkers were wiped out and that faction was just left there for someone to take there are endless resources. I can also use it to not take it easy and relax but also spread a more positive message for people to follow in Johnathan's footsteps.

I don't think any message would suffice. They won't believe any other message so I need to do it myself. Just giving a speech is not enough. I need to come up with a battle plan or some sort of confidence booster for them. To convince them they are enough to attack. To me it doesn't matter whether or not a lot of them are killed off in this battle because they are hypocrites and don't understand what it means to be a hero. Yes, I have killed people before and I have not always not done the most heroic things. However, I chose to evolve my mindset and become better unlike the rest. On both sides of this battle there will be hypocritical people, but I will protect the ones that aren't and after the battle is over the rest of us will prosper.

I grab a torch and since I am a lot taller than the average woman. I'm six feet and one inch tall to be exact. Therefore, people take notice of me.

"My fellow Chasers please do not be scared of The Stalkers! They are fragile and lost! Not as pure as they claim to be! I've been hearing rumors that they kept killing their own leaders due to a disagreement on their beliefs. Believe me I know. I have a plan that will take them down, BUT I NEED YOUR HELP! Cause a distraction for me as I sneak through the city. I will deal with the leaders of The Stalkers and we will take out everyone else. Once the leaders are out of the picture the rest of the faction will be under our control before the sun sets. To do that we have to avoid every other faction and go straight to them."

Immediately everyone starts to look excited and as if I've let a fire in their stomachs.

I best keep going.

"Once the city is ours! We will make sure that everyone will follow our values and beliefs! No more false gods! No more factions! Most importantly no more conflict within any of the land! Our writings, teachings and rules will make this world feel unified!"

Everyone is now cheering for me and is ready to follow me.

The cells doors have just closed and this wakes up all Anointed Stalkers. I brought them all here one by one with my mind control abilities.

They all look confused and agitated.

"Look time no see!"

Even though it takes them a few moments to realize it is me due to the restlessness they do recognize me.

I continue, "things are going to be a little different from here on out. We will no longer go after people to hurt them, but help them. You are all going to sit here and rot while I take this place and treat it as the most generous faction in the world.

We are going to keep on giving until the world no longer needs it. Get comfortable here while The Star Chasers kill the rest of your people."

One of the stalkers tries to grab me through the bars. I'm too far back for him to reach me.

"You'll get yours Nyla! These were your people too and you brought them to death's door!"

I go to the tallest tower and look out the window. I see a battle filled with nothing, but destruction and death. I want to help the innocents but that is not the most important thing right. Besides the fact that I see that people are fighting back using their powers to protect people. I want to use this battle as a distraction to start giving back to people.

The main way to do that is to go to the library and start writing my own stories about Johnathan. I need to pass on this positive image of him and that he is about helping people and not killing instead of this ruthless conqueror that just wants to take over everything.
Hopefully that helps pass this positive message more.

While on my way to the library I need to think of a pseudonym for myself. I can't use my name because I don't want to risk people not listening to me due to the fact that I was deemed as a traitor. Therefore, they could possibly disregard everything I wrote when they all figure that out.

Valeriana Samson. That will be the name I will be using in my writings.

As the battle goes on in the background I drive head first into the writing. While I write I look over some of the other writings that this faction has about him. I should really say hard because I will throw it all out soon.

I know a lot about his adulthood, but absolutely nothing about his childhood or teenage years.

Eventually the battle ends after three days of nonstop fighting and everything just goes silent. Within these three days I was also able to get a good chunk of writing in.

After all The Star Chasers left and went to another faction and all the mortally wounded were left here just to die I decided to go take a look outside at everything. There is a buffet of death. Dead bodies of men, women and children everywhere. Blood covers the streets of the faction so profusely that it's as if it rained blood. So much loss of life but none of it is in vain. People will look back at this moment and realize that with the benefit of reflecting on this moment it was a necessary battle that contributed to the greater good.

Whenever I got writer's block I would come back to all the dead bodies and bury them one by one. I take my time to bury everyone. I want to be sure that every single dead body is buried carefully and with respect.

With the writing I structure it as if I'm writing a historical account of the events of Johnathan's life. As if I was some sort of secret bodyguard for Johnathan that he did not even know was always there before he was even born until the day he died. Therefore, my writing reads like I'm an observer of everything and hopefully adds more of a believable sense to it all.

This routine of constantly writing and burying people goes on for what seems like months. However, to be honest it's possibly a lot more. I would not know because I have no one to tell me a clear sense of time because no one had come by here since the battle.

To take care of myself I eat whatever animal is left here. Dead or alive I eat it! Thankfully for fluids if I ran out of water there was a winery I could always go to.

With a, what I guess is a year of writing before I finally come with a title: A HERO AWAKENS.

What is also happening to me is that I'm starting to feel sick. How is this possible? I have unbreakable skin. How can I get sick if I can't take any damage? I mean come on when I accidentally cut a chicken's head off for some meat with a cleaver and I hit fingers and instead of bleeding it dented the cleaver. No way is this happening to me.

I continue to go about my business as if nothing is wrong. However, it is clearly wrong because I keep getting worse by the day. One day I keep puking every two hours.

The next I puke on myself and I shit myself uncontrollably.

Then suddenly I'm spitting blood.

I was wrong. I'm not impervious to getting sick. Externally maybe. Not internationally.

I'm dying. I can feel it. I'm convulsing and in so much pain that I can't let go of my stomach. Please make this pain go away somehow.

Once again I can see my lifeless corpse in front of my eyes.

NO! NO! WHAT THE FUCK IS GOING ON? I was back alive this whole time and I just did not know it?

PART 4

THE HYBRIDS

Chapter 22

Reborn again without even realizing it. How could this happen? Why would it happen? How easier would it have been if I came back and I just told everyone I would have returned? It also would be much simpler for me to conquer everything again. The thing that is the most frustrating to me is that when I wrote my own version of MY life story I would not be stressing out about details. I understand that either way they were targeting people that had unbreakable skin, but no matter what I would have kept my mouth shut.

I float up again, but not to the mirror dimension. I float up all the way up to the sun where I'm staring right at it. Therefore, it is staring back at me and starts moving while I'm completely still. A few moments later the sun is down and the moon is up. Then a few moments after that the sun is back up. This cycle keeps repeating itself ten times.

Then suddenly I get yanked away. It's as if someone has a rope around my waist and is pulling me. It's so quickly and so much force that I move so quickly that in a heartbeat I'm now in a completely different location.

I'm staying high above the sky looking down on a bunch of people. All of The Star Chasers have just finished fighting. As usual there is blood and dead bodies everywhere.

"The final faction has just been conquered." One of Star Chasers says proudly.

Then I get yanked somewhere else. In the middle of a wide open field. Once again standing high in the sky looking down on everything. I can see a bunch of different people with powers scattered all over the place. The sky starts spinning again.

Now I'm in a library of another faction. I can see a bunch of books being thrown into a random fire that looks like it was just started in this room on purpose. Someone else suddenly enters the library and notices what the other is doing.

"Stop it! What do you think you are doing?"

The person who is burning the books is in tears, "what the fuck does it matter, anymore? No matter how many rules we try to maintain. We kept our faith in him all the way but either way our faction fell apart."

Time suddenly starts moving faster again. However, I notice it this time by the fact that everyone is moving and talking faster than usual. It's like twice the speed of the average person. This goes on for a long while. This is only a guess however in real time it feels like it's been around a decade.

Yanked to the several different parts of the world and no matter where I am shown the exact same thing is shown. Chaos reigns supreme. There is no rule or anything anywhere therefore, everyone is doing what they can to survive.

This is why I should have been allowed to have my memories so I could lead everyone out of this chaos.

Now at random alley ways I can see a random man putting on a costume. Like a uniform it is black and blue and has the symbol of an eagle on the chest of it. He runs around at super human speed delivering some vigilantly justice.

Slowly as I get pulled in another direction I can see a bunch of people have taken it upon themselves to become vigilantes. This makes me happy and it means that my mission worked. However, this is not where I wanted it to lead too.

Eventually I arrive in a faction I've never seen before. The sign in front of it says, "Welcome to Equilibrium." While I float closer towards the front door I see a statue of myself destroyed and starting to rot away.

Wait! Am I back in Eden?

While looking into the place it still clearly looks like a place that needs a lot of repairs, but the only place is not burned to the ground. Majority of the same Star Chasers I saw before I see again here and now.

"No one will follow a false narrative about The Golden Guardian. Everyone will follow the appropriate one."

This is where they will start.

As the sun and moon continue to follow each other around and around over and over they rebuild this place to perfect. The resources, the architecture, the name has been even fixed.

Eventually the sky stops spinning and the sun has just come up. Equilibrium, which is now The Guardian's Hive, is beautifully rebuilt and ready for me to be born again and take it.

Their first course of action is to spread a message that they do want to unite everyone and have everyone live in one kingdom instead of a bunch of different ones.

They go around spreading this message through word and through their actions.

Their actions kind of work. They give food to the homeless and step in when people are being hurt, giving food to those who need it and countless other things.

Their words on the other hand are not working at all. As a matter of fact it is causing a lot of conflict with people. The most absurd part is not that they are believing in their mission. It's the fact that others don't want their mission to succeed. Everyone is used to the chaos not that they found comfort in it. Maintaining it is what matters to people.

Suddenly I'm pulled towards the armory in The Hive. Time once again runs past me in front of my eyes.

Every single member of The Hive looks exactly the same. Each individual has a different height, body mass, gender and so on. However, the way they are dressed exactly like me. Or I should say the superhero version of me.

They all have their very own version of the costume that they used to wear. However, a lot of them are not armored. Some are just made out of clothes for example.

"Stick to the plan everyone. We have to convince people that The Golden God is back. As we continue to help people in secret they slowly think he is returning and with all of our powers combined we can keep the entire world safe."

I'm honestly in such awe how much this kingdom evolved with time. Even though it has no king or queen it's designed as if it was made for royalty. The entire color scheme of the kingdom is the same as the one of my armor. Gold with a slight tint of black.

In a lot of the temples there are glass windows that each tell a story. A story about me that captures an exact moment of my life perfectly. Such as the moment of Kamar's death. However, not the most historically accurate. In the window it shows that I am the one who killed him and Charlotte is just standing there next to me. Also, instead of chopping his head off I'm shown stabbing him in through the heart. This is not good. The history has to remain accurate. I will correct them when I come back.

The pillars at every temple is black with golden lines on them. The lines look like pieces of armor.

There is not a single homeless person here or anyone who feels disregarded. Everyone contributes to this kingdom in some way, financially, educationally and any other way that can make the kingdom prosper. The goal is to eventually have everyone come here so that way there could be unity throughout the world.

Everything in this place looked so well polished from an archeological perspective that you would think that the rest of the world was not in complete chaos.

The way they decide to help others is by secret. No one will know it was them but they will also leave a symbol of wings after every act. To make sure they know, or at least think it was The Golden God. Of course no one wants to believe so they try to hide the symbol or kill The Golden God double that was there. Thankfully they were all able to get away, even if it was not easy.

Even though there are very minimal results for this part of plan they know it's not fast enough so they come up with a plan B. Make up stories about him coming back.

The way these stories were told was the old fashioned way. Just word of mouth. Of course the word did not spread very far because it did not make it far outside the kingdom. The next step was to start sending letters. There was no ruthenium to the way these letters were sent. They just had stories in them about me that were spread throughout the world.

Most impactful decision to help spread these stories is to write a book about them. One thing that I noticed about this book was that there was a lot of exaggeration of the truth. Every single detail of my life would be written in some of these books, but an exaggerated version of it. The most exaggerated part that I took note of was my birth. Instead of just being born with these powers they were given to me. These powers were given to me by some kind of extraterrestrial being after I was born. I was born just like everyone else and then suddenly at ten years old the sun shined on me for a little too long and I started to glow yellowish gold color. That's how I got these powers. These beings then left me here and did not give me anymore guidance just that I was sent here to save people and that's it. Furthermore, it was my parents that taught me how to do everything I know. The difference between right and wrong. How to fly, fight, and all my education came from them. Never went to school or did any other kind of education of any kind.

The title of this book is: The Golden Accounts.

This book was passed around all over the world. Whenever one of the members of The Golden Hive would do a random act of kindness they would "accidentally" drop a copy of this book. Therefore, someone else would pick it up and read it and the word would spread with momentum.

However, one particular case of someone grabbing a copy of the book is that when I am forced to observe then they change the narrative to fit their own ideas of them. This continues to happen over and over the more the book spreads all over the world.

Then all of a sudden I realized that just made everything clear for me. The reason I keep coming back whenever the world needs me to come back. Therefore, that's why I can't choose my own abilities because I am given the abilities that are needed for me to make the world better, how it's supposed to become better, not how I want it to be better.

I finally know what I have to do. The final question remains, how do I do it?

Chapter 23

Well I've noticed that I can't decide which powers I get. That's the first problem I'm going to have to solve because I won't be able to help anyone until I know which powers I have and how to use them.

The second problem is one that honestly has me more concerned about how I can help people if they have an automatic rule to kill everyone with unbreakable skin. How can I be helpful while being hunted and have a giant target on my back?

Whether or not I have my memory back it does not matter because either way I always learn how to use my powers for good anyway so I'm not concerned about that.

Honestly though, I'm asking myself the wrong questions here. Not what I want to do to help them? What do they need me to do to help them?

Well something that I noticed the more time passes be is how much they use entertainment to tell my stories. Even though some of these retellings may be complete bullshit, it is arguably more of a domino effect than anything else to spread my stories.

Especially with this new thing called motion pictures. Every motion picture made us different from the last. However, that unfortunately creates a horrible sense that every single person is trying to pander to a different group of people. Instead of telling the story. The way I'm presented in these motion pictures generally shows me as heroic, compassionate, intelligent and many other consistent characteristics. That's fine by me. What I'm not fine with is the fact that every actor that is chosen to play me is chosen out of popularity. Furthermore, the race is changed constantly depending on who the motion picture is made for. Also, it looks like depending on the audience watching each motion picture one of my characteristics stands out more than the other. If it was an audience filled with children I looked much more heroic. If it was made for adults I'm much more intelligent and much more if violent tendencies are shown. Also, physically I keep changing and appealing to whatever is needed. Two motion pictures come out about me only four months apart. In one I had blank hair, blue eyes, and with white skin.

In the other I was bald, with black skin and incredibly short.

The world has evolved so much that I can't even recognize it at all anymore. There are no kingdoms and factions anymore. Now there are countries and continents. Technology has evolved to the point where we no longer need horses. We have auto automobiles now.

The only thing that has stayed the same is that there is one work ruler now. However, this person is not the King or the Queen but a president. That's what they are called now apparently. Thankfully there has not been a war in hundreds of years and the unity was kept. There are still crimes of course. They are all over across the world. However, it's never escalated to something past that.

Watching how much in love people became with me due to those motion pictures I realized that when I come back I have to figure out a way to create the perfect image of myself. I need to figure out how I can appeal to the image of myself physically so that everyone is happy with the way I look. Everyone welcomes me back and is put off by my new appearance.

If I'm going to focus on giving people what they need instead of what I want to give them I must figure a way to give back to them. Give back to them non-stop and equally as well. However, that's something I can't do alone. I need to have a team of people that shows me how this goal can be achieved, but at the end of the day I made the final decision on everything.

The one world president that exists can work. I just need to know that this person can be trusted. Furthermore, can this one world government be trusted? Even if I keep a close eye on the current president by the time I can actually return it can be a brand new president that no one should have even been given the title.

Being in the president's home is going to show me the exact reason why I need them to achieve this goal when I return. What I mean by them is not that I need this specific individual's help, but the help of this government. How I can use it when I come back and what to do with it.

This president's name is Cornelia Wulf. She is in her third term as president. It has just started only one week ago. In this one world government the individual can run for president as many times as they please and can win as many times as the people want them to win.

There are just a couple of conditions that every single person who is running has to have to qualify to run.

The first is there has to be no criminal history of any kind of the person who is running. It could be a very minor crime like getting a parking ticket when you were sixteen years old. You are automatically disqualified. The reason is because this crime stays with you forever like a record and the person who is going to be the president has to look like a perfect citizen that everyone can look up to and follow in their footsteps. Therefore, any kind of crime you commit before someone can take inspiration and repeat it. No matter how minor, no possible bad messages can be sent from the one world president to the people.

The second is that you must be a hybrid. This means that you cannot be someone that is born from two super powered parents. Or born from two normal parents. The reason is there cannot be any kind of bias for one over the other. Therefore, you must be someone who has a parent who has powers and the other who does not. However, this is one little loophole. The parents don't have to be biological either. One can be biological and the other could be a step parent, or even an adopted one. Also, if you come from a background of mixed parents you also understand what it is like to live both lives. That's because you may have power, but you also understand what it is like to be human and have the human experience while also having the superhuman one. Therefore, you find a good balance between both and you find a way to help everyone in a fair way.

Cornelia is celebrating with her family. I'm assuming it is her adopted family. Along with her husband and child. Her parents look very different from her. Cornelia has red hair, green eyes and is short. Very short, no more than five feet and two inches tall and white skin. That's with heels. Both mom and dad are at least a foot taller black hair, brown eyes and brown skin. Her son is no more than thirteen years old and her husband is only a little bit taller than her. Five feet seven inches to be specific. Blonde hair and blue eyes and he also has white skin. His name is Reed. He looks like a very big and buff dude. As a matter of fact he looks so big and buff to the point where I noticed that whenever he walked anywhere he had this blocky pace to his walking. To the point where every step he took it sounded like he was purposefully stomping.

I slowly get yanked to follow Carolina and Reed to the cemetery. A fresh bouquet of flowers has just been placed next to the tombstone.

Kara and Josh Parker are the names written on the tombstone.

"I finally got justice for the man who killed you both. I hope you are proud of me."

Reed looks at her, hugs her and kisses her head.

"I'm sure they are."

I get yanked super quickly to a sudden place in a desert somewhere. I'm clearly on the opposite side of the world and it is so dark out that I can't see three feet in front of me.

Suddenly a bright flame lights up right in front of me. This flame is not just a tiny little light from a torch. This flame is the size of a person. A seven foot tall person that is dressed in fireproof clothing. He then suddenly takes flight and glides around the skies as if he is on patrol. As he is flying through the sky his flame lights up the area around me. There are a bunch of different people around me. All have their own unique super powers and their outfits complement those powers.

I can see them all getting up from resting a little bit and continuing their job. Their job is to be a protective military that looks after everyone and steps in and stops crimes when they need to.

Now I'm in a much richer part of the world. I can see that people with superhuman abilities are using them to make things more convenient for everyone else. People with abilities such as superhuman speed and flight are used as a form of transportation.

Being yanked back Reed he is in a random building just cleaning the floors. There is a team of cleaners in this building both male and female. One thing that I noticed about all of them is none of them have powers. These are the people that look the unhappy. Not because they have a terrible job, but because they feel like they are just living a life instead of choosing a life.

I'm forced to follow Reed around for a long time and due to the routine he does daily it is clear he wants to be a part of the military not a part of the cleanup crew.

He workouts every day. He constantly learns new fighting styles and studies military strategies throughout history. It's like he plays with the belief of a military general whenever he is alone in his house. It's sad really, it's like he knows he can never live to his full potential because he is not allowed to. I've noticed that when he is with Cornelia he pays so much attention to everything because he wants to learn as much as he can.

In these meetings even though there is a one world government there are still leaders in all the other countries. Each individual country has their own leaders. They all report to the current president how things are going and how things can be improved. I know I've chosen to let go of wanting to be the one in charge. I'm just really bothered how black and white they think all these can be solved.

Everyone that has these simple jobs like cleaning does not have any super powers. My guess is as to why these jobs are given to these people because they don't want to disregard everyone. However, it does not change the fact that a lot of them feel neglected.

These are the people I need to help the most. The ones who feel lost, without a purpose. However, here is my biggest fear. Due to the fact that the law that anyone with unbreakable skin is to be killed I can't go about this mission in any way I please. At least not alone. I need to work with someone to achieve this goal. Not just because it will be easier to accomplish this goal, but also because I hope that I can convince myself that I'm here to help. Therefore, it will result in them not wanting to kill me but instead use me to contribute to making this one world government better.

PART 5

THE BEARER

Chapter 24

"This is how you respond to your hero coming back? With public execution?"

"Are these your final words?"

"You can kill me now, but I promise when I return you will regret turning against me. I was generous in this lifetime, but I won't be in the next. I guess in a way I should thank you. Finally opening my eyes to the truth. You are all inherently good. However, you lack the strength to give instead of take. You lack direction. Don't worry, in the next life I will show you all the proper path that you are supposed to be on. All of you will be corrected."

I say all these words with disappointment in my voice. The disappointment echoes throughout the world because everyone is watching this execution. I know because I was told that my execution will be broadcast worldwide.

One thing about my execution that confirms to me that they only want me here for as long as they can use me, is the way the execution is being played out.

Instead of just finding a simple way to execute me and deal with me quickly, they purposely pick a slow and painful execution.

This form of execution is similar to getting the electric chair but far worse. It's a chair that when you are put into it you are strapped down then a bunch of needles start moving towards you.

Each needle goes to a very important spot in your body. The kidney, the heart, your lungs and so on. Then a fluid goes through these needles. This liquid goes into these areas and obliterates it. Each organ that this liquid goes into shuts down and you feel the pain of that. I've never felt more agonizing pain in my entire life. Thankfully I don't have to put up with this much longer because I can feel my soul slowly draining from my body. As this happens my life starts to flash before my eyes. To be honest this life feels like nothing, but a complete waste. However, I have to stay focused on the lessons learned in this life. Not on all of the things that I did not want to happen in this life, but the things I need to carry with me into the next one.

I was born in the year twenty-four fifty five. A really big jump from when I saw this world last. Well over one thousand years since I was last alive, but also a good additional two to three hundred years at least since I was just observing it.

In this life I am given two powers. The first power is the ability to manipulate people's minds. I can't control anyone, but I can get them to think they see certain things even though that's not actually there. However, the only way I can manipulate their minds is how they see me. What I mean by this is that whenever I look in the mirror I see myself. My real self. The Gold Goliath. The version of me that is entirely made out of gold and that I have unbreakable skin, and that the black outlines give a perfect texture to all of my muscles. Along with the white pupils and gold eyes. Everyone else sees someone different. I mean that literally every single individual person sees a different version of me. I can see the real me, but my mother for example only saw the human me without any armor, tall, dark and handsome. My father saw every man when he looked at me. More average height, average build and nothing special. The way I know each person can see a different version of me is how they describe me. I'm not talking about how they would describe me personally. Whenever, someone would mention how I would like someone else or try to draw a picture of me, whatever it would always look different. If I denied it they would get mad and think I'm lying. The most bizarre part about the entire situation is that whenever I got my picture taken with a camera or a video that is the only way they could see the real me. That was the only way I can prove to people that it was the real me. That I was actually back. The way I use this power is not really even by choice, it's like it just happens, like an instinct. It's very similar to how a person breathes. They just do it without thinking. Even if someone looks at me without me even knowing it I look different in their eyes. Lastly, it did not matter what age I was either. Everyone saw a different version of me whether I was five, fifteen, or fifty five.

My second power was also the thing that saved my life. I have the ability to magically just give people what they need. I mean that in a literal way. Whatever, someone needs metaphorically or literally that I give them so I can help make their lives better. This power was presented to me from birth. My mother, whose name is Susan, in this life was infertile and they tried nonstop to have kids because it was her dream to be a mother. She actually wanted to be one more than anything in the world. According to my father, whose name is Gregory, on their wedding day she wanted to have at least five children. That's why when I finally showed up after them trying to have a child for over fifteen years they thought it was a miracle. That's why ever since my birth they will protect me no matter what they will always protect me.

Thankfully though all of my memories are still here. To be honest though I'm not sure how accurate they are anymore. I'm officially thousands of years old and it's impossible to remember everything that has happened to me, but I do remember the most impactful moments of my life, although the details might sometimes alter whether I intend to or not. If only I could also have the ability to remember all my memories to the most specific detail.

Although I do look like my golden self I don't have any other abilities. No wings, no flying. No super human strength and no unbreakable skin either. I was able to figure this out by one day accidentally cutting my finger while slicing bread. I did not bleed profusely. Nevertheless blood did come out of my finger so no unbreakable skin.

Regrettably I did not start going to school from a young age. I actually skipped school because of the fact that I still had all the skills I learned before. I was still educated and willing to learn everything new there is to learn here. However, instead of learning it through school I decided to learn it through the streets.

Even though I was back I decided to not announce it to everyone and had my parents promise to not tell anyone either. The reason is that before I decide to deviate my time to collaborating with the president and helping the world I want to make sure that I'm doing it on my terms.

To not draw too much attention to myself I helped people in a way someone would expect someone of my age to help someone.

At the age of six I would people the way a six year old would be expected to help people. If I was ten the same thing would happen. My very first act of heroism was at the age of six.

That was really when I noticed how much this world changed since the last time I lived in it. It's been well over one thousand years since I was able to draw a breath, and because of that I never felt so much relief since I drew my last one in the previous life.

Technologically the world is way more advanced than before. Even more when I was just observing it.

A lot of vehicles are still used because they don't drive on roads anymore. They just hover slightly above the roads.

Therefore, this means that cars are the main form of travel. There is no other vehicle needed. The cars will take to the places that are even in another part of the world or across an ocean.

These vehicles look completely different then the way they did before. Now they look like spheres. The colors of the spheres depend on each individual vehicle. However, the colors are reflective spheres that everything outside and inside the vehicle can be seen. Whenever the vehicles crash into each other a sudden armor comes over them to protect them.

The reason there is such a low amount of vehicles in this time period is because there is such little need for them. The majority of people have continued to use their own power as a form of travel. Whether it is flight, super speed, teleportation and so on. However, there are still laws to make sure that even follows some rules when it comes to transportation to make sure that no one gets the impression that certain people are treated more favorably than others.

Those are the same as everyone else. Speedsters have to be careful of their speed limit, same with flyboys and girls. People whose form of transportation requires some kind prepulsing to activate, such as using their fire powers to fly, need to be at safe distance from everyone else before they take off.

Unfortunately though these laws are not helping as much as they should. There are still countless people that die in accidents unintentionally. People with certain powers can use them as a job to transport people to different locations. However, there have been countless deaths because of it. People with super speed would move so fast that people they were transporting their heads would fall off. This is one instance of hundreds happening on a monthly basis. They eventually banned people using their powers for transportation because of this.

No one is allowed to use any powers to aid anyone else in any way. Unless they were trained to do it or they were given the authority to do it legally. With proper authority from the government and everything.

Because there are so few vehicles all over the world, there are many more houses and places for people to live in. Homelessness is practically non-existent.

The houses are very different as well. They are made from the metal that my armor is made out of. Apparently only one hundred years ago they were able to reverse engineer my armor and figure out what material it was made out of. However, the material changed depending on which armor they looked at.

The armor from the first life I lived is very different from the armor in my second life. Therefore, depending on which house someone bought, that's the kind of material the house itself is made out of. On top of that is the price, of course.

Apparently while I was still alive and the older I got and the more of my armor started falling off or crumbling away. People would find random pieces of it and keep it. They would treat it like a souvenir.

While other pieces were just found in random places on the ground or the ocean or wherever. As time went on some of these pieces completely decomposed. However, some pieces didn't and those were the pieces used to help build houses.

The more they reproduced the more they could use to build houses.

The more material reproduced the more houses that got built.

Every single house has its own unique color to it, but whatever color the house has inside so is the outside.

The houses themselves don't look like regular houses, but they look like mini temples. The architecture from the outside looks like they are trying to protect something. Therefore, that is why the metal on the outside is a lot tougher. Even though no one can tell.

The rest of the world looks entirely digital. From the roads, to traffic signs, to everything else. Therefore, because everything is digital it adjusts accordingly. For example, when it is snowing the roads become warm enough which results in no ice forming on the roads.

My heroic act at the age of six started at the local playground in my neighborhood. I would walk to the playground on my own because it was only a two minute walk from my house. You could see it from my bedroom window. I would walk to this playground on a daily basis just to hangout and hopefully, eventually come across someone that needs help.

Eventually a boy by the name of Steven Yu. He ended up being the first person I helped. He would always come to the park very late at night with his mother. They would always come here late at night after his father was asleep.

The reason they always wait until the father is asleep is because then they won't have to worry about his temper and drinking issues. These issues came from a great sense of jealousy.

This jealousy came from the anger he feels towards the people who bought his company. Steven's father started a company that was selling security systems to people. The company was successful enough, but he was no billionaire by the time he sold it to some other people.

When he had enough money to retire he sold the company to other people who turned it into a billion dollar enterprise. Therefore, a lot of spite built up in Steven's father. That formed into alcoholism and abuse. The reason was simply because it was someone else and not him.

I knew this because every time I saw both Steven and his mother they looked physically and emotionally hurt. They did not have to say a word, I could just see it. The actual details of Steven's father and what started all these issues I got from him.

Surprisingly enough his mother never really stopped us from talking. After all the information it's like something in mind snapped. I can't really explain it, but suddenly it's like my body got taken over by a puppet master and I was doing things that I needed to help fix Steven's situation.

The main thing I have to fix is Steven's father. He needs to be out of the picture. Things have to be this way because no matter how I try to get Steven's father to go on the right path he won't listen. To me it honestly looks like he does not want help. Steven told me on multiple occasions where they tried to step in and help him, by starting interventions and even bringing in friends and family. However, he would not listen as a matter of fact he would get worse. In his father's mind the moment you look wounded or weak in any way you are a bad person. Therefore, no matter what was done he would not change.

Also, after his father was gone there was a clause in his contract that twenty-five percent of the royalties from every sale that the company makes goes to his son once he officially has a bank account.

In the long term that was a big benefit to me because Steven made a promise with me that after he and his mother was set free he would repay me. He meant this in a literal way because after he created his bank account he would share his wealth with me. Both he and I never worried about money ever again. I also got a friend for life after the day his father died.

On that particular day I did not go to the park, but I waited outside his house. I found out where his house was because my dad in this life is a cop and he gave me the address. His house was only a twenty minute walk from me so I just wanted to go there. While walking there I kept a tiny little screwdriver in my pocket.

I noticed that thunder was starting to rumble in the clouds so I moved a little faster.

When I got to his house the driveway had one car on it and I could see the father just drinking inside the house from a window.

I throw the screw driver at the window. The impact is hard enough that it shatters the window. The father immediately noticed and he started coming towards me. However, he clearly is very drunk so he stumbles around while moving towards me.

Therefore I start to run slowly away. Slowly enough that he sees that it was me but not to the point where he could catch me.

Then I see him getting into his car and moving towards me.

"OH SHIT!"

I couldn't help but scream those words out. Not because he is coming after me and might catch, but this guy is not just angry, I think he is willing to kill me for breaking the window.

All right, don't panic, I need to stay focused. So what do I do now?

Oh right! The lake. I can lure him to come to the lake and hopefully he is drunk enough and stupid enough to drive the car into the lake and not get it in flight mode.

Thankfully that is exactly what happens. At this point is pouring rain and on top of that the slippery roads and his drunkenness causes the crash. However, while the car is slowly drowning he does turn on the flight mode. That being said, still being drunk he stupidly crashes the car into someone else's house. Not a dent is on that house or the car, but the moment he hit the house it's like the car just stopped working and it just slammed on the ground.

I ran back home to not risk anyone else seeing me or connecting me to this incident.

Things did not get any better for him since that incident. He drunkenly confessed to everyone therefore he got arrested. The trail went by pretty quickly and while he was in prison he got killed because his temper got the better of him. He would get into fights and arguments all the time. This got him locked up in solitary confinement and eventually shanked for his aggressive behavior.

After this both Steven and his mother were in a great state of grief and at the same they were a lot less stressed. Not just because his father was not here anymore or the fact that soon they will have a lot of money, but simply put they felt free. They felt like they did not have to worry about someone constantly looking over their shoulder.

Steven's mother eventually found another spouse and she has been a lot happier since then. Steven himself felt relief more than anything.

"I'm not concerned for me or my mother's safety anymore."

Chapter 25

Steven and I have stayed friends for years and the older I got the more I looked more like my original self in the eyes of everyone.

Even though Steven protected my secret and along with my parents tried my best to deny all the rumors it was becoming near impossible. Therefore, I had to leave everything and go on my own.

I had two bags with me. One filled with food and other necessary supplies to remain safe. Another bag completely filled with money from Steven.

I tried my best to help people while trying to live a more traditional life to connect more with the people. I felt like I needed to do this because it feels like I forgot what it is like to feel basic human things that everyone experiences. Relationships, exploring the world and countless other things.

The problem was that I was no longer able to keep my identity a secret. Everyone was gravitating towards me. It was at this point I realized that I regretted not going to school. I don't regret all these experiences I had, but none of them will lead to connecting with the world on a global scale.

Only way I can connect with people is through individual one on one interactions. I can't help as many people as I need to even though I have given each individual that I helped exactly what they need. It just felt like I was not communicating that I am here to help everyone.

That's where the regret of not going to school earlier on came in.

If I made myself look more qualified I would have been able to be more transparent about it.

Next thing I know I'm in a university doing all the school necessary to prove myself to the world. At first I needed to do a bunch of upgrading. I never went to any other schooling of any kind so I had to start from kindergarten level education when I applied. However, thankfully I went in the levels fairly quickly because of the fact that I used all the schooling I had from my past lives. Therefore, they were surprised how much I already knew.

The thing is though since I'm an adult now I look like my original self in the eyes of others. I stopped feeling this sense of fear. The reason is because the more connected I become with people the more I am able to help them.

Therefore, the more welcoming they were.

Although maybe a little too welcoming. They were constantly trying to get me to do things for them. Favors should be giving them money, doing their work for them, helping parents take care of their own kids and a bunch of other basic tasks that they don't need.

It was never that I did not want to help them, I did not need to help them. At least not in that way they wanted me to.

The university I went to helped a lot. You learn things really quickly there. They just put a helmet over your head and the brain just observes the information. Depending on how much you pay that depends on how fast you finish everything.

I went to school for political science and law. This helped me get really caught up with the world today and how things work.

The one world president rule is still here. However, now there is no limit to how long the president can stay in power. As long as the people chose for them to be in power a long time. When they vote for which president they want they put down two things. The person who they want to vote for and how long they want them in power for. When the voting process is over whoever had the highest votes wins, obviously. On top of that though whichever time was chosen to be the most selected for the candidate that's how long they will be in power. These rules are also completely set in stone. This means that if the candidate also wins a ten year presidential term then that's what they must serve. Unless of course something happens to them. Such as them dying young or a criminal record as countless other reasons. The amount of time they can serve is decided by all the votes counted for the current president and will be the amount of seconds they will be in power.

There are countless experiments to help ordinary people get super powers because normal jobs are not really needed anymore. The reason is because even if people with powers do those jobs instead of people without them they are accomplished more sufficiently.

Speaking of people with powers depending on what powers people have they are automatically guaranteed a certain job. People with superhuman abilities are guaranteed jobs in firefighting or police or anything related to police life work depending on which they choose.

People with superhuman flexibility are given jobs in the medical field.

These are just a couple of examples, but of course no one is forced to do these. It's just a more granted path to success.

Unfortunately this has resulted in a "sleeper" battle between people with powers and people without them. They are both fighting for jobs and therefore, there is a battle between them that never ends.

This also resulted in people without powers looking for ways to get them. Even if they wanted to get them illegally they found away.

Crime has gone up unfortunately because of this and it is still able to be maintained, but for how long? I need to find a way to be in the oval office and be the helping hand of the current president.

Andrew Pollock was the current president of the world. He has a vice president named Francine Hayas. They have both been in office for about eight years now. They both have super powers and they both come from interracial families. That's more than any other president in the past, from what I learned they are focused on making people feel united.

My original plan was to finish school, get a job and slowly be on my way. However, the day I graduated from university I got arrested. It was on a bullshit charge just to find a way to in prison me because everyone became too afraid of me. I wanted to resist, but that puppet master sense of control came over me and I just surrendered.

Chapter 26

Chains around my wrists.

A bright red jumpsuit on my back.

A windowless room is where I am. Therefore, I feel like I'm starting to go mad.

I'm not sure how long I've been here for. However, I can feel the sense of time pass me by how much my facial hair is bothering me because of how much hair there is. On top of that my hair is touching my shoulders now.

I was put in this room because I caused so much distraction. Indirectly, but they blame me for it so they say I caused it.

The problems I caused were so severe that I got sentenced to death. I was just waiting for the official day of execution at that point.

What caused me to be thrown in here was that after I got arrested and I was officially all over the news people had a very split reaction to my return. This caused countless crimes to occur all over the word. As a matter of fact it was the highest crime wave in centuries.

People I helped tried to help me constantly. Protesting for my freedom while in here. Trying to help me escape even while I'm in court. Holding police officers hostage with their own guns and demanding my dismissal. However, no matter how much I wanted to escape, that puppet master power took control and kept me there. I needed to be there. I needed to be here and help others.

Others constantly wanted me dead. While in prison I got into several fights because I had a target on my back. I fought a lot of them off, but others got lucky, and I would be stabbed or knocked out from an unexpected attack.

I kept my faith in what I needed to do and it paid off. I realized that what I needed to do was be transparent to people.

I was much clearer about my message.

My group of people I kept as friends was smaller, but we were a lot closer.

The message I gave to people was much more positive. My goal was to help people. Never harm or cause them any harm. No killing, or commuting a crime for the sake of a means to end. Even if it is in the name of heroism.

This resulted in a lot of prison riots because people motives to fight in my name and do what they think I would want.

More prisoners that were easier targets in the cells now had more protection from other inmates. The more violent inmates had more people standing up to them and this made the entire prison go into chaos.

The prison I was sent to was called The Super Cube. Everyone in here had a superpower and depending on the color of their jumpsuit should show how incredible of a power they had.

White jumpsuits meant that their powers were not really a problem at all. It was just their actions that led them here. An example is if someone has superhuman intelligence, but their power does not harm anyone directly then it's not a big deal. However, if they still committed a crime using it then they are put in here.

Yellow jumpsuits are people whose powers they used to commit a crime. A man who had the ability to teleport from one location to the next used his power to go into a bank vault to steal money.

Red ones are people that their powers can cause the most amount of damage to people whether they realize it or not. In my case my abilities allow me to influence people in any way I can to get them to do whatever I want them to. However, I don't have that power. They just think that is what my power is. I know it's them just trying to look for new things to complain about even though there is nothing to complain about.

That puppet master feeling would constantly come over to just protect others and spread messages about what I want people to do.

Eventually the entire authority side of the prison got control of everything again and that's why I was locked up.

At first they did not want to have me executed. They tried to get me to use my powers of giving back to people what they in the way that serves them personally. I tried my best explaining to them that it's not how that works.

That's when everyone started getting more violent and aggressive towards me. Trying to force me to use my power in a way they want me to.

No matter how violent they got, nothing worked, but that is when I learned my lesson. Nobody actually wanted my help. No one actually wanted me to return unless I helped them in a way that they felt was convenient for them. Of course when you do that then no one actually knows what they want therefore you can't really help anyone. Therefore, that's why I can't work with anyone anymore. I have to work alone and stay focused on how I need to help the world and not tell anyone what I'm doing.

The worst part about the entire execution is the fact that my parents were there. They saw me die.

Being back in that dimension now I look back and I know I helped a lot of people. Whether it is with something small like standing up to a bully, but others I completely changed their lives to the point where they are doing better like Steven. Of course I did the typical hero stuff like stopping crimes, but now I know I can't just help individuals anymore.

No matter how many people get hurt in the process. The goal is to help fix the entire world. Therefore, now more than ever I need to focus on going on my own path, not worrying about what anyone else says, and not worry about what might hurt people with what I do.

From this moment on it will literally be me against the world.

PART 6

THE WANDERER

Chapter 27

All my powers are back. I mean my original powers, the ones I've had in my first life. However, this time they are more advanced than before. As a matter of fact more advanced than all of the previous times I had these powers before.

That being said though I do need to test them and see what my limits are. What are the maximum limits that I can push for my flight? I don't have wings again, but can I breathe in space? I don't know, I guess I'll see.

I just need to figure out how to get into space because it is separate territory.

Once it was New Year's Day in the year three thousand, space was losed off to everyone else except people who had permission to go up there. There are multiple ways to achieve this of course.

The first to become qualified to go up there. Astronauts are the main occupation that makes you qualified of course. Secondly is deciding to take on another profession that requires you to be in space all the time. Dimension seeks is the name of that second profession.

This profession is made to look for my "home world." Obviously it does not exist. However, everyone is convinced it does. Since I'm the first "superhero" I must have done it somewhere or something else. It is not possible for me to just have been born like everyone. I must be from another world. That's what created this program. Therefore, that's why space is closed off for everyone else. They want to explore other planets in the galaxy to find the one that I'm from and destroy it. They are not saying that out right to everyone, but I know that's what it is for.

That is because whenever they claim they "found new life" on the new planet they always claim that whenever they get there some sort of fight always breaks out that results in the planet getting blown up.

That is how I will be able to get to space. I will enlist in that program and I will be able to explore.

While out there if things work out in my favor I will start taking steps to test the limits of my other power: superhuman strength.

The thing is though ever since I've returned everyone is super nice to me. I'm not stupid I know for a fact it is too good to be true.

That's why I'm over thinking every single thing I do. I know they have eyes on me everywhere. That's why I know I can't just go into space and they will just be ok with it because there will be some sort of catch to it.

"Yes, no worries, you can just fly into space."

"Oh. That easy? Ok seriously what do you guys want from me?"

"What? Can't we just be happier that our savior is back?"

"I guess so?"

I say that with a very suspicious tone in my voice.

As I fly in space just exploring it and realizing I can breathe in space and fly wherever I want without the sense of danger on my body. Also, I don't think I have any speed limits on how fast I'm going. I can see multiple planets zooming past me within seconds of each other.

Which also confirms that my unbreakable skin is back. However, there is no sensation on my skin at all when I'm in space. Not just in space, but with anything. When I hug someone I feel nothing.

When I kiss someone I feel nothing and even when the wind blows I feel nothing. I can always hear it, but never feel it.

While I continue to fly throughout space I can't help but have this gut feeling that something bad is going to happen soon.

This is why I need to figure out the limit of my powers. I know I can't count on anyone else to be on my side so that's why I have to be able to protect myself. No matter what the cost of everyone else is. I don't want to come back to another life. This will be the life I will achieve my goal because I don't want to have another couple of hundred years go by and completely reestablish everything I lost.

I know it is only a matter of time before I do something and their entire fake loving peaceful scam is up and they try to kill me again so I need to hurry and figure out all of my powers and all of my limits.

Ever since I was born in this new life everything was just so easy for me. It feels like everything was just handed to me at the most convenient time when I needed it.

When I was born, mothers who were going to give birth to pure blood shower powered babies were kept in a specific hospital. The Kamar's health miracles hospital.

After I was born and people realized who I was, they did not know what to do with me. As a matter of fact they did want to kill me, but they couldn't. My unbreakable skin stopped them. Even when they tried harming me internally, by feeding me poison nothing worked.

Therefore, they just kind of left me alone. My theory is that they left me alone just for me to not suspect anything. I'm sure they have some sort of contingency plan for me if I do go crazy.

That's exactly what I will use to take advantage of the situation and use my strength.

Slowly as I fly down back into earth from space a sudden vision manifests into my brain. A vision for this world and I'm going to take it. I will not only test out my strength, but I will show them in this test there is nothing they can do to stop me achieving my goal.

NO ONE IS GOING TO STAND IN MY WAY!

The way I will put my strength to the test is by stopping crimes mainly. I will not harm anyone innocent because if I do then I will make innocent civilians afraid of me. I don't want THEM to be afraid. Only those who NEED to fear me.

At the speed I am now with how I'm flying it looks like I'm just gliding through the air.

I look around for crimes to stop. Situations to test my strength. I keep letting my eyes wonder for seconds that turn into minutes.

Finally I see an armored vehicle being chased by armed robbers in another vehicle. I fly right into the vehicle filled with criminals so hard that it instantly flips into a building. Thankfully no pedestrians were hit because everyone moved out of the way on the sidewalk and then the car just went slightly into the building not too much into it that it went right through it.

I land softly on the ground. I take a couple of steps forward closer to the car. The car itself looks completely totaled. When I hit the car it was hit so hard that some of it looked folded inwards from the dent.

The first robber was dead on impact. His face was smashed into the car door window. His face looked completely cut up from the class. The top of his head was cracked open from the hit on the glass. Then some of the cut up pieces sliced his face up. He continues to bleed out even though he is dead. The other robber is looks like he is bleeding a lot too. However, he looks a lot worse. Due to the impact it looked like all his bones broke, some even were sticking out. His arms and legs look twisted in an insane way. He looked at me as if he was in complete shock and in great pain.

I could see his eyes. They were clearly saying help me.

I just simply shock my head no.

In an instant every single person there cop or otherwise instantly pulled out a weapon and pointed it right at me.

Without hesitation they started shouting at me. The bullets hit me like rain hitting an iron railing. The bullets don't hurt me at all, they actually deflect off me. Some even bounced back at them. A bunch of tears fall from my eyes while I'm being shot. I knew this was coming, but to turn on me instantaneously? To go from giving me whatever

I want to wanting to shoot me dead I am truly heartbroken. I know they were against me for thousands of years now, but how dare you try to stop me from trying to prevent evil things from happening.

I thought about the surroundings, but it's no use. How can I test my strength on these people? I'm not mad at them directly because I'm sure a lot of them are following the laws that are given to them.

Then all of sudden these people are attacked from nowhere. These attacks are not by people using guns but people using superpowers. Surprisingly though no one is killed everyone is just hurt or incapacitated.

After they have taken everyone down. A woman who lands right in front of me as she makes herself land with the electricity that she can produce from her hands. She stops flying and starts looking at me up. She looks very tall and slender, with blonde hair, green eyes and white skin. She is wearing normal clothes. As a matter of fact all the super powered people.

"My lord! Come with us!"

"I'd like to know who you people are first."

"My name is Shannon Nickels. We are the descendants of everyone you helped over six hundred years ago."

I instantly snap back at her.

"That's not enough information. How do I know you guys are not lying?"

Shannon says comfortingly, "This is going to be a long story."

Shannon takes a deep breath in, "I'm a descendant of Steven Yu. Ever since he started having children he dedicated his time to preparing us for your return. At first it was just him, his wife, Anna and his two children, Bruno and Bruce. However, the more time went on the more people we found. The way you helped them resulted in them wanting to dedicate their lives to you. This has gone on for centuries and eventually where got things entirely dedicated to your name. Temples, radio stations, shops and so on. If you come with me I'll explain more along the way."

I felt hesitant because I did not want to feel used, but since they mentioned Steven there has to be something to their story.

"Fine. For now I'll listen to what you have to say. However, if this turns out to be a trap. I will kill you all."

Shannon is clearly taken aback by what I said. She actually looks very offended. Her mouth is a little hung open.

She takes a couple of moments to collect her thoughts once again.

"Then I have nothing to worry about."

Then all of us take off. I follow Shannon to wherever she wants to leave me while the others follow.

The others use their way of traveling while Shannon and I fly side by side. Everyone around me looks like they know exactly what is going on except me.

"Where are we headed?" I ask hastily.

Shannon replies with a smile, "Back to your home of course."

"Eden? Or The Golden Hive? Or..."

"It has a new name now. The Golden Pound is the name that was given to The Golden Hive almost five hundred years ago."

"How many people are there?"

"Plenty! I don't know the exact number but we are no more than one million."

"That is how many people have been waiting for my return?"

"Oh, you have no idea. Every single person you helped in your previous life automatically did something in return that was used as a tool to return. This is the thing though they never even had a choice. After you helped them, suddenly they felt possessed to prepare for your return. For example, after you helped a woman named Rebecca Hamilton, she used her gift of education and leadership to start her own educational program that only talked about you and educated people about how you affected the world and the true history of who you are. Plus she did the same with children. Here is the most bizarre part though whenever any of them had children it was passed on. This passive feeling of doing your will. It's like it was passed on genetically."

"I appreciate everything you're doing for me. I need to stay focused though. I have to do this alone."

"My lord... with all due respect... we are a part of this whether you like it or not. There may be a lot of us, but each day more of us die. Kamar's descendants are always after us."

"What are you talking about? I thought that they think we are all allies."

"Not anymore."

"Can you elaborate, please? I don't know anything that happened behind the scenes, honestly."

"How could you not know?"

"I was so focused on myself that I stopped paying attention to the world around me. The only things I focused on were the tools that were going to help achieve my goal of world peace."

"My apology, I guess you wouldn't know because they kept it all hidden away from you. Their true intentions I mean."

"So my superstitions were correct?"

"Well I don't know I'm not in your head, sire. That being said, if you are talking about the fact they want you dead one way or another, but they hid that from you by being overly nice, then... yes."

"I never understood why anyone thought I was ever related to him. That was never true."

"I never believed you were. That's not what matters though. What matters is what everyone else believes."

"Which is?"

"Around three hundred years ago Kamar's descendants figured out that you too were not allies, but enemies. Therefore, the rest of them dedicated their lives to killing off your descendants and you. Of course all of this is done in secret. So it's like a "sleeper war" as we started calling it. Also, what I mean by killing you it's not just that they want to kill you in this life. They want to kill you permanently to the point where you never come back and you are whipped from the history books."

I listen to everything that she is telling me and this is why I don't want to have anyone helping me. I don't want anyone innocent to get hurt in the crossfire. On top of the fact that I know it is only a matter of time before they turn against me because I won't do what they want me to.

I need to find a way to get Shannon and the rest of them to fear me. To stay away from me and never have any other by my side ever again. I and she just fly past a prison.

Suddenly I get a sadistic thought in my head.

I'm going to fly right down there and kill all the prisoners and do it in such a grotesque way that they will all be repelled by me.

A bunch of people are working out in the fresh air.

I fly straight down as fast as I can.

"Hey! Wait! Where are you going?"

I slammed straight into a man that is there lifting weights. I land so hard that it makes a small hole into the ground and the sound of a mini earthquake is heard. He looked crushed like a pancake.

His blood and bits of flesh are all over me that I actually had to wipe it off. Especially my feet. I had to use my fingers to take off the bits of flesh off my feet like mud.

All the other inmates around me are so shocked that they are all completely dumbfounded.

I walk over to the dumbbell rack. As I take each step it sounds very metallic. My footsteps always made sounds that sounded metallic since the day I was born into this new body. The thing though on this floor in this prison they sounded specifically like two cans hitting each other.

The prisons slowly start to snap out of the shock and try to run away or get the attention of the guards.

When reaching the rack I go over to the heaviest weight. Its one hundred and fifty pounds. I pick it up as if it is nothing. I'm picking up a leaf off the ground.

Then I threw this dumbbell right at one of the prisoners. It hit him in the head. It partially fractured his skull and he is starting to bleed. Good.

I then pick up a three pound barbell. I pull it up right. Then turn my wrists and push straight up. Three hundred pounds and still feels like nothing.

I throw it at the front door to block people off from exiting. Some of them try to fight me while others try to just keep away from me.

I fight them all off while also killing each of them one by one. Snapping the necks of one guy. Punching my fist right through their chest in another. So much death so quickly that it feels like it all happened in a flash. My golden skin is strong that whenever someone lands a punch on me their bones in their hands break instantly.

Behind guards are heard running towards me. Above me Shannon and the rest have just left me here.

The guards don't just have a bunch of weapons for me but also a bunch of robot bodyguards as well.

They try to attack me and wound me, but nothing works. However, I'm not attacking the guards back because I know these are good people. I mean their job title even clearly signifies that they are dedicating their lives to helping others.

My hands are up.

"I don't hurt other protectors!"

One cop shouts at me, "On your knees! As a matter of fact, face on the ground!"

"I'm not going to do that." I respond very softly.

Another cop cuts in, "He wasn't asking, ASSHOLE!"

"And I'm not requesting."

They all of a sudden start trying to attack me and they start to dog pile on top of me. I can easily break free due to my big size. I'm once again over seven feet tall and around three hundred pounds. However, I'm not sure how I can break free without hurting any of them.

If only I could make a copy of myself. If only I can have two of me or even three I can move them all off of me.

Suddenly I start vibrating and then suddenly two different copies of me just start peeling away from me. Once they are out of me they do exactly what I tell them.

We'll all suddenly just fly up and observe each other.

We all look exactly the same. We all think exactly the same because it's like all of our minds are linked. Furthermore, we can see each other from different perspectives. I should say I can. It's like I'm just hopping from eye sockets to eye sockets seeing what each person can see.

We all put a sudden series look on our faces. We all say in unison, "let's go kill the rest."

Smashing right through the ceiling of the prison we kill off each of the criminals. The also cool part is each duplicate of me has the same abilities.

"I need more!"

Once again we speak in unison. A split second later our bodies start vibrating and more duplicates tear apart from our body. However, not just the source but from each of us. It doubles from each duplicate two more are here.

At one point a duplicate that is at a completely different part of the prison where the others are he can hear someone talking, but I'm nowhere near him. However, I can hear that person as if I was the one in that part of the prison.

"Please spare me, almighty one. I may have done bad things, but I was desperate and afraid. If you give me another chance I will dedicate my life to being by your side."

That duplicate rips the cell door open and holds out his hand, "I am taking your word very seriously. You better prove to me that I made the right choice. If not, you will suffer."

Even though I said those words in the back of my mind I never mouthed them. Neither did the rest. That one particular duplicate is the only one who speaks. So I can also direct my voice to which duplicate I want? That's going to come in handy.

While going through the rest of the prison I can clearly see how strong I am however I can't find the limit to it. To be honest I don't think there is one.

Rescuing that random inmate made me realize that before I go around killing every criminal I need to figure out who all the good people are. In particular I need to figure out who all the people are on my side and choose to be part of my utopia.

All of me kills all criminals and then just flies off into space just floating there. Waiting. Thinking. Contemplating my next move.

Chapter 28

I can't believe I never figured out I had the power to make duplicates of myself. I'm surprised I never figured it out before. Never really needed it before, I guess. Since someone of my size never really gets challenging or really even talks back to me I never thought about it. More specifically there was no one I wanted to hurt. At least not yet.

How wrong I was when I felt like Shannon just abandoned me. Actually none of them actually were working on a contingency plan for me. To cover up for me whenever I acted violent. For the first time in thousands of years I actually felt like a king again. With the prison fight they are spreading a new version of the story that a prison riot was started by one of the inmates and that I went there to help.

Nevertheless I need to stay focused on my goal. As my body vibrates and more duplicates of me get created I think more and more of how I need to get as many people as possible to listen to me. I may be killing a lot of people soon, but that does not mean I can't spare as many as possible. The thing is through a lot of them are telling false or exaggerated tales about me. Therefore, I need to tell everyone the truth once and for all. At least tell it to the best of my ability. Yes I may have all my memories of my previous lives, but I don't remember everything to the tiniest detail. Like what food I had each day, or how many times I took a shit.

Every duplicate travels all over the world to deliver my message.

Millions of eyes all over the world to observe it. How beautiful it is. The unfortunate thing is that once I finish stating my message it will all be gone. Worldwide war will be here again... very soon.

Landing in a very crowded part of every city, town, village, and street that was very crowded with loads of people. Making sure that a lot of eyes are on me I take a deep breath in and start to speak.

"A lot of you believe in me. Unfortunately not a lot are told the real truth about me. A lot of stories have been fabricated about and I want to be honest with you all. Not all of you will be happy with what I have to say, but it's the real truth. I was born to normal parents just like the rest of you. Unlike the rest of you I was born with abnormal features. Wings that grew out of my back and metallic gold armor that was hidden underneath my skin. I don't know how I got these powers. To be honest I don't know if I ever will. That being said I always felt this sense of responsibility to help others and give back any way I can with these powers. That's exactly what I did for a long time. I had my doubts at first if it was actually going to work and if people were actually ok with me doing it. My parents talked about my heroics and never complained about it. All they worried about was my safety. I had one rule for myself and that was to never kill. That was very hard to keep, but at the same time I felt like I had to live up to an image. Heroes are supposed to help people. Constantly give, but never take. That being said, that was building up a lot of anger in me. Anger that I had difficulty fighting and anger that I felt ashamed of having. When I did finally snap and started killing I felt relief like I did not have to hold back anymore. I always wanted to start killing some of these criminals. Some of them were such rotten people that it is honestly a complete mystery to me how they ended up that way. To be honest I did not care at that point because I was so angry with everything else. All of the lives lost and innocent people damaged beyond repair just so I can look like the hero everyone wanted me to be. WELL FUCK THAT! I'm tired of doing 'what I'm supposed to do.' I'm going to do what needs to be done and what needs to be done now is that all bad people need to die for all the good to be spared. All of that follows me knowing you have no need to worry you are spared. Those of you who are descendants of Kamar's bloodline. The stories are not true. I was never related to him. I actually fought him in battle and I helped bring him to the woman who killed him. I know you are just doing what you are told by others and following your beliefs. This is why I don't blame you for following false gods. That being said, I am offering you your one and only warning. This is your chance to turn your back on the false gods and follow me. If you don't you will be left behind with the rest."

PART 7

THE DEVOURER

Chapter 29

No more than an hour has passed since I gave that speech. It spread like wildfire through people's ears and everyone instantly started going crazy.

Before fighting in the war I had to be a protector. The reason is because I started randomly killing each other, in particular the descendants of Kamar started getting killed off. There was no discrimination who in terms of who was being killed. Men, women and even children weren't spread.

Me and my doubles stepped in and protected as many as we could. We actually had to kill some of our own people because they thought they were trying to kill innocent people.

Shann's people came and helped and took all the people that needed protecting away to safety. I knew it was Shann's people because they all appeared with costumes that looked exactly like my armor except they were all latex and had wings in the center of the chest of each costume. Like a symbol.

Each individual person who was taken to safety were taken to The Golden Pound. The majority of them were people with no powers, but quite a lot of them were with powers.

The people who had powers had to be taken to safety because they all had powers that would not be very beneficial for a war.

What I thought would only take no more than one month ended up taking almost a year.

Bring people to The Golden Pound. Finding ways to keep them safe and taken care of. Making sure everyone had shelter, food and all of the resources required to live.

Even though I do need to do this alone I'm not going to turn down help from the people who want to help.

If they want to be a part of this final way, so be it. I just want to make sure that they are compatible. I don't want to lead people to their deaths that would have been better just to stay out of the battle.

It's a win for me. The more people fight alongside me the more enemies will be killed off the quicker the war will be over.

Plus if I lose a lot of soldiers then the less people I'm going to have to look over once I rule this place once again.

This may sound like a very selfish thing to say, but honestly, its how I feel. I think that was honestly my mistake when I was originally king. There were too many that I had to look over there that's what caused the mistakes that echoed through history.

I kept a bunch of different doubles all over the world to keep an eye on specific things while I prepared for war.

The first couple of doubles were kept in The Golden Pound. They were there to make sure everyone was kept safe and fight off any soldier from the opposing side that possibly got through.

Another group of doubles was helping get weapons for the rest of the soldiers that did not get powers and wanted to participate in the war.

I'm going to kill anyone I come across on the opposing side while we are preparing for the battle because I want to be fair and give as much time to people as possible to change sides. Literally until the moment before we start marching towards each other, people can change sides. Everyone else is dead.

Everyone who does have super powers did not want any armor. Even though I kept telling them they should get some. I guess they could be seen as one. I won't be able to protect them that well because I have to keep my focus on the fight.

The Golden Pound is located in a completely isolated part of the world. It is actually located on an island isolated from the rest of the world to protect it. It is being protected from being taken over by anyone else but me.

Apparently that is what I was being told while I was trying to get all the people to safety.

The rest of the people who did not join me, but also did not want to partake in the war are hiding in their homes. Afraid for the coming battle, but their choice has been made. If at any moment their mind changes and they join me I will spare them if not then I will leave them in the hands of fate.

Chapter 30

I have doubles all over the world. Both sides of the army have soldiers all over the world. I meet with the leader of the opposing army right at the center of the earth.

The leader of the other army's name was Nox. He is the last direct descendent from Kamar. He is also the current world president. He always kept an eye on me. What I was told the night before the battle is that he was the one who ordered me to try to poison me. He started all the secret wars and contingency plans to kill me if needed. Apparently even if I tried to educate myself more on him and his plans because his people were doing the exact same mine were. The only difference was that they hurt me with the resources they had.

He has a particular grudge against not because of who I am, but what history reviled for him. When the truth came out that Kamar and I were enemies not allies it caused a lot of divide between our two bloodlines. Therefore, when was married to one of my descendants she left him in a heartbeat and he held that against me for the longest time.

I can't begin to imagine how much hate he had for me at this very moment. It's not your fault that you were told a false history.

I thought like the last time I was in war we were going to discuss terms or some sort of conversation... nope.

Guns just started basting.

Fists started flying.

This is going to go on for a long time and there will be a lot of collateral damage.

Shooting fire blasts at each other, throwing each other through buildings and just causing so much destruction that it felt like the end of the world.

Even without seeing them actually die I never knew everyone who did not go to The Golden Pound.

I did warn them after all.

It is also a very bloody war because depending on which ability people used on others their deaths would be more deadly.

People with superhuman strength would crush the heads of others.

People with superhuman speed cut people up like butter.

I would run through people like glass or pick them up and let drop from a high stance to kill them.

Sometimes to make them suffer a little more I would fly them up to space and leave them there.

The most brutal kills I saw were the ones with people who had the ability to move things with their minds. They would literally rip people apart.

The most amazing thing for me was that whenever someone tried to use their powers on me they just didn't work. They couldn't use it on me. Someone who has the ability to move things with their mind simply does not work on me. Never knew this was possible before, but now they don't work. My guess is because this is one of the abilities I was given with this new body. Here is the most bizarre part: their powers don't not in sense they don't have an effect on me. It's more the fact their powers literally just shut off whenever they try to use it on me. Of course they would turn back on the moment they used them on someone else.

This actually resulted in people starting to surrender in different parts of the world.

One by one they all stopped fighting and dropped their weapons.

Some of them even started to bow to me.

Nox was the one whose goal to kill me never changed.

When he realized that everyone was starting to surrender he gave it his best shot and took a sword and ran right towards me to kill me.

I sigh at him and when he runs towards I grab his head from behind and rip it right off.

I hold it high like a trophy. Blood spills out of it

"The war is over! A bunch of you already surrendered to me. It is however too late. You already made your choices, you took his side not mine. Therefore, a lot of innocent people died as collateral damage. You all will die because your selfishness and pride killed them."

Those words echo all over the world due to where all my duplicates are.

I instantly threw the head across the street and started to kill the rest of the soldiers who survived. If not me the rest of my soldiers did.

PART 8

THE OVERSEER

Chapter 31

Every single soldier of Kamar's army has just been killed off.

There are countless dead bodies all over the world that result in the entire planet looking like a bloody graveyard.

All of my duplicates that are on the island go over to a blacksmith. He is ordered to make a crown for every single duplicate. The black smith does just that.

While the crowns are being produced he every single dead body is being disposed of.

I walk over to the building to where I was originally born in The Golden Pound. Now, of course it is not that exact building, but this building is located in the exact location I was born, which is my original home. I walked over to the exact spot I was born. I know this is the exact spot I was born because my mother would constantly repeat it to me. After all these years she has said it to me so often that it never left my brain.

A good renovation is what this place needs. Currently this does not look like a location fit for a king. This looks like an average house that anyone would live in. That needs to be changed.

After getting all the construction workers and telling them how I want it changed I had a sudden realization. Once this place is finished being renovated I'm the only one who has to be able to get into it. That's more of a safety precaution for me just in case anyone else decides to turn against me.

"The house is going to be located in space."

They all look at me very confused and I just simply say, "Did I stutter?"

All of them give a miniature bow.

As the bodies were being disposed of I realized that it was not permanent. It was like garbage just because you put it all in one spot does not mean it is permanently gone.

Then suddenly looking through the eyes of a different duplicate of me I see that one of my soldiers throws one of the bodies into a wood chipper.

That's the permanent solution. We all take the rest of the dead bodies and put them all through wood chippers or really any machine that allows you to cut anything up into tiny little pieces. So tiny in fact that none of them are recognizable. The rest of the remains of flesh and blood and everything else is cleaned up. All put into disposable bags and thrown out of the planet by me.

It's as if none of them existed and they will be completely forgotten about in time. As for all the people who fought on my side are being buried properly. We make sure that all of our dead are gathered first and then let all of their families say their goodbyes before burning them.

While they were being buried I came to a sudden realization. I can't just let them be buried randomly and just leave it there. I want their grave sights to be legendary and be echoed through eternity. I could have won this war completely on my own. In a way I have, but I don't want to come across ungrateful so the burials themselves have to feel more like rituals.

First thing that was done was that coffins were individually made out of the same material that my wings were made out of. Since that material was constantly reproduced and used by everyone I took pieces of it and made coffins out of them.

Paints came in and turned them gold. Then the bodies were put in there and they were buried. However, they did not have tombstones with dates of birth then death. What was actually done was that once they were buried they would be buried in the exact spot they died. In the ground there would be an engraving of their name, birth and death date and a symbol of a pair of wings. On the wings there is a second engraving that says, fallen wingman. Or if the person buried is a woman it would say, fallen wing woman.

After we buried everyone the next step was to completely rebuild the world. All the damage that this war caused will be fixed and better and stronger than ever.

All the while my place was being built as well. They had a long staircase leading up to the house. The stairs were painted in pure gold with black out lines on them. This makes the golden tile on the floor look like there is a clear separation between each tile and each title looks like it is the size of my foot.

I walked up those steps to see how long it would take.

Around the time I got to the top of the stairs it was at least a good hour.

Stepping inside the house, it was clearly not finished yet. That being said, it does look like it is coming together nicely.

All that matters now is the painting and the hardwood of the house. Of course also the decorations.

With the decorations I want them all to be memories from the past life. I don't want to forget any of them. Especially the important ones.

A portrait of Charlotte along with all the children we had together.

As people enter the place if they can reach is to see a painting of me during my first war. Flying above my army as we charged towards the enemy.

All of these memories will be painted in a goldish, yellow color. The rest of the house will be in green, from top to bottom.

Finally once that is complete there is going to be a barrier around the stairs that will block any other way for people to come to my home unless they climb those stairs one at a time. The barrier also is narrow so only one person can climb at a time. That limits the amount of enemies I'll have to fight just in case they start turning against me anytime soon.

As for the way that the entire world will be rebuilt it won't look newer than it did before. It will just look polished. The reason is because no one wants things to change, they want things to be the same. Just with all of the bad parts erased. If that's what they want, that is what they will get.

Chapter 32

The world is finally rebuilt and at peace. Everyone is listening to me finally. Surprisingly the fear of being attacked is not in the back of my head as much.

All the eyes I have around the world looking over everyone never saw anything suspicious.

Thankfully this gives me the opportunity to find the key to stopping myself from dying. I don't want to come back again after any other one thousand years or whenever the fuck it is and have to take the kingdom again for a fourth time. Hell even more times for all I know. Out of all those powers that were given to me I never could see the future.

First thing that I have to do is figure out what my weaknesses are in this body. I know I'm invulnerable, but it just seems too good to be true. There has to be something that can hurt me, or take away my powers. I'm going to find it no matter how long it takes.

There is no typical man made things that can harm, so that is crossed off the list. Aging? To be honest that affects me too. It's been twenty-five years and the world is still being rebuilt and when I wake up in the morning and look in the mirror I don't look a day older. My armor and powers have not been downgraded or affected in any way due to the fact that I'm older either.

Ok, so aging does not affect me. What is my weakness?

By the looks of things I need to figure that out sooner rather than later. People are starting to not appreciate the peace. That's no problem, I'll just kill whoever commits the crime.

I will be fair. Six year old's robbing a gas station with a candy bar, no. It is not a crime punishable by death. However, if someone invades someone else's house then, yeah. No hesitation about what is going to happen to them. As a matter of fact I'm going to make sure that everyone sees what I'm doing to make sure the people see what the consequences are for their actions.

With a rope around the necks of a group of wanted armored truck robbers, while their eyes get more and more bloodshot and their last breath is about to be drawn, everyone is looking at them in horror.

I'm hanging them in broad daylight and up high in the sky in the middle of the day because I want to make sure that once they die they will be dropped splat on the ground like a tomato. Everyone will see the blood and hopefully this scares them into stopping. Even though, of course I know it won't.

That thought proved right as time went on they kept throwing things at me, shooting at me, trying to stab at me, and hurt me in any way they could. Nothing is working, but this means that more people have to die.

I fight back and kill a lot of them. This gets some of them to run away and some are now even more motivated to get me.

Nothing seems to even affect me in any way until someone makes a custom knife made out of the same material as my armor. I'm assuming that they got it from their house because their homes are made from similar material.

When that knife goes through my back it hurts me. I scream so loud at the top of my lungs that it echoes through the earth because all my duplicates scream from the pain all at the exact same time.

This is not just hurting me... This is killing me. I can feel it. The specific duplicate that managed to throw a knife into my back, actually killed me. I can feel these duplicates like defeating him. However, the others are not affected by it.

When that duplicate dies I kill the rest back to me and ask the other closest live duplicate to pick up the dead one.

They all reach my home, for the first time in a long time I feel fear. The people found my weakness and now if they wanted to they can kill me.

I don't want to give up on the people, but I can't stay here because even though I made it as hard as possible for people to reach this place, sooner or later they will find a way.

Even though the duplicate was only dead for a couple of minutes it already started to decompose. When I pull the knife out of the back of it, liquid pours out. I'm assuming it is blood, but it does not look like blood. It looks like honey more than blood. It's yellow and thicker than blood, but when I touch it clearly feels like blood.

Unfortunately I need to think of another way to help them. Clearly being too ruthless is too much for them this the third time I made this choice and the same thing happened every time. I need to do better.

At the same time I don't want to have to die again and restart. What should I do?

I look around the room just letting my eyes wander as my brain cooks up a plan. All the while one of my duplicates looks out of the window and sees people trying to find a way up here.

Another duplicate looks at the dead one and then at each other then it just hits me. I know what to do. I know what plan I will put into action that requires the perfect balance of being able to keep all the progress I've made. However, at the same time it will convince people that I feel guilty for what I did and that I'm changing my ways.

> Step 1: Bring all the duplicates back to the original host, except one.
>
> Step 2: Grab the knife from the dead duplicate, then stage this house to make it look like I just lost my mind and plan on killing myself. To make it more dramatic I'm going to fill the house with gas and blow it up.

Step 3: Go out there and slit my own throat with the knife. Once one duplicate dies the other will go out into space to hibernate so to speak.

Step 4: Once the hibernation process is over I will come back and continue to help people.

As this plan starts forming in my head my duplicates are already destroying the house. Another one looks out the window seeing the people back away out of fear. Finally another goes right over to the stove and turns it on.

Then slowly the rest of the duplicates slowly return to me. It feels like just putting on a jacket you have not worn in a long time. You have warned it for so long that you forget it exists.

I pull the knife out of the dead duplicates back. While at the same time the only duplicate left looks for a box of matches, a lighter or anything that starts a fire.

After waiting a couple of minutes the duplicate hides in a corner while trying to start the fire with a lighter.

Lifting the dead body and holding it in my arms like a barbell I slowly fly towards the front door of the house.

The exact moment I open the door the entire house blows up. As I fly slowly towards the people the duplicate flies higher in space. No one saw him.

Everyone has their eyes on me, "I see that you are all very unhappy with me!"

I drop the dead duplicate on the group and it makes a giant thud.

"I'm sorry that you don't see me as your hero. I'm sorry for being too harsh to all of you. Killing so many of you. Therefore, I've decided to kill myself."

While speaking I'm pouring all of my emotion into it and tears are in my eyes. They are buying it.

I stab myself in the neck on the left side of it and pull it all the way to the other end. As I'm bleeding and dying I can see people screaming in fear and crying because of what they are seeing.

PART 9

THE MANUFACTURER

Chapter 33

While Johnathan is floating high above the planet just contemplating what to do next the people back on the ground are taking the dead corpse of the throat cut duplicate and disfiguring it.

However, there are others that are protecting it. Therefore a fight starts to break out.

At the same time Johnathan is vibrating his body again to make duplicates. The duplicates are multiplying enough that they all make a circular around the earth.

Suddenly... Everyone has stopped fighting back on earth. While they were fighting over the dead corpse some of the blood from it went on some of the people. Therefore, it healed whatever physical issues they had. Even if it was a small drop of the blood on them it was healed. It heals the physical illness no matter how severe it is.

Some of these people had small zits, scars and marks that were healed. While others would have lost limbs grow back.

Then a group of people pick up the body and carry it to the nearest hospital. They dissect it and try to harness it as much as possible.

In the meantime back up in space Johnathan thinks of a new way to help people. He knows he can't be a tyrant. However, at the same time he can't be a side kick to the people either. He needs to figure out how he can be a helping hand for the people, but at the same time do it his own way.

He then sends a couple of duplicates down to earth. As they split off from the circle more duplicates appear to close the circle again.

He goes back down to earth, first to a random clothing store and takes some clothes. The clothes he takes are a long, thick, baggy hoodie, and a pair of sweatpants that are also thick and baggy. Shoes that have an incline to them and the bottom of the shoes have a design to them that makes them perfect for slippery roads. The inside of them have fur in them and they keep the feet warm. The colors of these pairs of clothes and shoes are black and white. As a matter of fact when you zip the hoodie up the zipper goes all the way up to the head and it looks like a skull. The entire outfit from head to toe looks like it is the layout of a skeleton.

He is able to take the clothes and sneak out of the store without anyone noticing him. The reason is because even though this is a place that looks pretty new, it's as if it was suddenly abandoned.

Although Johnathan was flying away he did not notice the dead people at the other part of the store who were clearly attacked and killed.

Some duplicates are around the world just flying around looking at everything. The duplicate with the clothes is much more hands on. Even though the clothes are making him stand out he was not trying to stay incognito either. He just wanted to make sure that no one knew who he really was behind that hoodie.

Therefore, when he sneaks outside the store he does not fly out. He just walks out. While outside he finally noticed why that store looked abandoned because on the outside of it everything is destroyed.

Cars are on fire. Dead bodies in the street and blood everywhere. The most horrible thing about it is the fact that these people were not just killed they were completely dismembered. Some are torn apart, ripped into pieces and their blood is leaked completely out of their body.

Other duplicates see this happening all over the world. In particular this happens to only people who have superhuman abilities. After being torn apart a lot of them are being eaten, or people are just drinking their blood.

Johnathan has no idea as to why this is happening. All he can do is just step in and fight people off. However, he moves so quickly that people see him.

He flies right through a group of people so quickly that no one even notices what happened. The man with superhuman ability to stretch his arms out was not even paying attention because he was so scared. He just checked up the roof of a nearby building to escape.

Covered in blood and guts now the duplicate looks for other people to help while staying incognito to make sure no one realizes who he is.

All the duplicates do this while the one in the skeleton uniform keeps a closer eye on things.

Chapter 34

The purge and consumption of the super powered people goes on for months, the majority of them are almost extinct. Few that are left are in hiding, keeping their powers a secret.

While the rest of the world is cleaning up the mess everyone else is slowly returning to their normal lives.

In time a new world president was elected and slowly the world started to prosper again. However, in this new world there was an automatic law against all supers. They were all automatically labeled outlaws. They are to be captured at any coast but never killed to harvest their blood.

With so many supers dead and the rest on hiding everyone starts to slowly move on and this results in people starting to forget about them.

The new world's president has a name, Benjamin Ritter. He is a president that is doing everything that is required of him to give hope to the people and get people to work together again.

He ends up being the president for exactly thirteen years, five months, twenty three days, eight hours, nine minutes and twelve seconds. The reason was because the people suddenly wanted change and it was given to them with a new president, Alicia Claiborne.

Observing this from afar finally realized how he has to change for the people to accept his help. He has to adapt to what they want him to be while still doing things his way. He will turn himself into a hero that people want him to be, such as the way his costume looks, his abilities, his motivations and so on. Until whenever they get bored of that hero, or he is killed or whatever ends up happening to him, he will come back and become a different hero that the people want to see.

Johnathan knows he can't do this alone so therefore he has to look for people to help him. He searches for the rest of the survivors with superhuman abilities.

Chapter 35

The first super that he finds is Shannon. She hangs out in a small town called Wingtown. It is a very peaceful place with a very low crime rate and beautiful scenery. This is a town located near the mountains with a lot of senior citizens here.

Shannon is here enjoying her peace with her husband and children. He was able to find this place because of all the duplicates circulating the earth.

Johnathan does eventually find the rest of the supers round the world. However, when he goes to recruit them only one goes to do it. To maintain the illusion that it's a new version of him instead of the same one.

He goes to her in secret in the middle of the night while everyone else is asleep except her.

"You're still alive? How is it that you are still alive? I saw you slit your own throat that day."

"I came back."

"You look exactly the same. I thought you would look different and more evolved than last time."

"Well you look older."

"Yeah that happens."

"Listen, I came back here because I need your help."

"I'm sorry that can't happen. Even if I wanted to, if they figured out who I was they would kill me and my kids."

"I'm guessing they all have powers?"

Shannon nods.

Johnathan continues, "Then how come your husband did not say anything?"

"Because their powers are not anything crazy. My son has the ability to change his eye color and hair color at will. While my daughter can change her height at will. We and the kids are able to keep it secret that he won't suspect anything. They only started to develop at the age of fourteen so they were old enough to understand."

While he is talking to Shannon he's talking to others as well. Surprisingly a good chunk of them accept Johnathan's offer pretty quickly.

They decide to help Johnathan in any way their skills can contribute to the plan that Johnathan has. Even if that skill is minor like being good at baking they use it.

Every skill contributes so that way whenever Johnathan starts being a hero again he can have all the resources necessary. Back to the bakery example they will make food specifically that files him up faster or food he can carry with him to give to the homeless.

Every single duplicate is given the proper resources needed to look for them to appeal more to the country that he will be helping.

Johnathan back with Shannon has just left and she goes back to sleep after looking at her children once again.

The next day while giving a live report on current events suddenly she is suddenly interrupted by the ear piece.

"Shannon, please meet me in my office."

"I'm in the middle of a live broadcast."

"I'm aware." The voice in the ear piece continues. "That doesn't matter, just meet me in my office now."

Shannon does exactly what she is told. When she comes to the office instantly two cops hit her with batons right in the back. She goes straight down.

"WHAT THE FUCK IS THIS?"

Police officer, "you are under arrest for having superhuman abilities and hiding them."

An instant look of fear and sadness takes over her face. She knows what this means. Her children and the entire life she has built is gone. She is so distraught that all she could do is cry and speak under her breath, "Johnathan please save them."

All the cops and as a matter of fact all of the law enforcement officials are humans now. Machines are only used to handle jobs that don't require it. The reason is because now that people have started to slowly forget about heroes over the last few decades, people want to feel connected to normal people again.

Johnathan is not aware of what has just happened but one of the other supers who works with Shannon and that she is unaware he has powers he passes this information on from person to person. Eventually it reaches a duplicate and Johnathan is aware.

One duplicate goes after Shannon and the other goes after the kids. Both duplicates are dressed the same. One is dressed in a spandex costume that covers him from head to toe. The other while also having a costume that is coming from head to toe is made entirely out of Kevlar armor. Also, costumes have the skeleton scheme to them. Once again the skeleton made a perfect outline of him, but the shoes also had feet.

The reason Jonathan chose this skeleton scheme to show people that he conquered death and that he will bring everyone else to it sooner or later if they continue to commit crimes.

The duplicate with the spandex goes after Shannon and when he reaches her he smashes right through the car. He smashes right into the top half of the car. He cuts through it like butter and sends it flying. He then goes back to the back seat and gets Shannon out. She is still a little out of it and has whiplash.

"I got you. Don't worry your kids will be safe. A friend of mine is picking them up now as we speak."

There are other cars around him all filled with law enforcement officials. They all had their guns pointed right at him.

He flies straight up and they fire right after him. He purposely uses his body to cover Shannon up.

In a completely different part of the city the Shannon's two kids are hiding in the corner. As Johnathan is killing off all the people who tried to bring harm to the children. The children are still in hospital gowns and some of them have small scars that the staff just started carving.

After killing all the staff he brocades the door and gets bandages to put on both of them. Then he takes them all away.

Shannon first is dropped off at the top of a mountain. This mountain has a bunch of people on it preparing things for when Johnathan is going to become a vigilante.

"Stay here. Your children will join you soon. Go to the medical tent to get any medical treatment you need."

Johnathan flies away now.

This location in the mountains is like a personal hiding ground for Johnathan and the supers. More importantly this is Johnathan's own secret layer so to speak.

This mountain is older than Johnathan and everyone else there. It's around two million years old. It has a lot of flowers on it and grass. However, what is particularly important to take note of is the fact that these mountains are goldish yellow. All the rocks around it are as black as the night sky.

It was found by the Stanley family who used it as a safe haven. They started building a life here and eventually built some small village for everyone to live in. Johnathan found and instantly they became allies. Ever since then they have used this place to give Johnathan everything they become and in turn Johnathan cured all their illnesses. The husband had issues with diabetes that were healed. The wife had issues with dementia and that was healed and their daughter had issues with asthma, which is now non-existent.

This is the reward that Johnathan gives to anyone who helps him. Make his heroic mission accomplished and in return you will be healed of all physical and mental illnesses you have.

Everyone here contributed to the vigilante goal that Johnathan wanted to accomplish. Each individual has their own job they have to do, but at the same time they still have the ability to live their own lives. They have houses here, food and every other resource to live a sustainable life. A life that they feel and not a worry about their safety and fear of being attacked.

There is a security team that looks after this place twenty-four seven because of the duplicates. Even though Johnathan still needs to do basic things to survive such as eat, sleep and so on. Not all of them need to sleep just one duplicate and the rest get what that one got.

Suddenly a different duplicate lands on the ground with Shannon's two kids. She runs right up to them and hugs them.

She looks right at Johnathan. She does not have to say anything; she expresses all the gratitude she can convey.

"Sorry I could not save your husband. He was killed because they assumed he knew something and whenever he denied it they hit him. They ended up beating him to death. You have my condolences."

She starts to cry again. However, it's not loud, just a silent one. While she hugs her children tighter.

"You have my support for your mission from this moment on. As long as you promise to always keep my children safe from this moment on."

Johnathan nods.

Chapter 36

A solid year goes by. Everything is finally prepared for Johnathan to start his vigilante mission.

Everyone is in position, doing the job they are required to do.

Johnathan is standing on top of a rooftop on top of the highest building of each city each duplicate is in.

Every duplicate is dressed in costume with the Skeleton scheme but each costume has its own unique appeal to it. Appealing to each culture that each duplicate is in. All of them have their masks off.

"Ever since I could remember I always wanted to help people. However, even though I realized how to help them I never realized the most important aspect of it. This is something that never has a finish line. There is never a point where I can stop helping. This is something I need to keep doing forever. This is something that requires constant adaptation. People need help. There is always someone that needs help. Not everyone can be saved because I can't save everyone they want to be saved.

What I can do is make sure that I go out of my way to protect everyone to the best of my abilities and make sure that the crimes are not repeated. Kill everyone that commits a crime and make sure that individual never can become a problem for anyone else ever again. I can never tell anyone who I really am besides the other supers who I can consider really close to me. I can risk repeating the mistakes of the past whether I'm directly held responsible for them or not. From now to the rest of eternity I will protect and help as many people as I can and I will whatever adjustment is needed to keep that promise. Now and always. With this current superhero persona I have to be a hero who has no powers and relies on normal weapons to stop crime and protect people. While having all the resources in the world needed to help those at their convenience. In my next superhero persona I don't know what I am required to be. All I know is that it will turn me into something the people need."

While this quest echoes through Johnathan's mind he sees sirens and emergency vehicles moving around. He puts his mask on and jumps off the building.

REFLECTION

This is the very first novel I've written. Technically, the second of you includes my Novella, Concubinus.

It honestly started to become a little frustrating for me that it took so long to write. I want to be clear I'm not complaining, it's just more of a shock then anything. Although I did learn one valuable thing while I was writing this book.

That's to just go where the story leads you. You can't force things to happen. I originally finished the book back in July of 2023. All I had to do left was just a final edit. That is where I reread the book and I just make changes as needed. I thought that was going to take me no more than a month. It ended up taking me almost five. From July 2023 to November 2023.

Now that I am officially finished, I can't let this frustrate me anymore and just kind of let things be.

Currently I have two ideas for novels I'm writing. One is called Transplant and the other is called Chains.

Transplant is a science fiction, mystery and psychological thriller. Chains is a gothic paranormal romance. From the stage of development I am now writing them I don't think they will take long to write. They both are not very big novels and are not on an epic scale like this one. However, I don't know which one will be finished first because it depends on how much inspiration I have for each individual idea.

Now that being said I could be completely wrong. I may finish both at the same time, or very close to each other.

That's why I don't ever put sneak peaks of my next book in the current. How can I give you guys a sneak peek of my next book when I don't even know what it's going to be about.

AFTER DEATH has charged so much from the original idea that it was a completely different genre now than before. The only thing that stayed consistent was the title. The book was originally a historical fiction book about me being friends with an historical figure and how that affected me. How would being best friends with someone like Napoleon or Alexander the Great affect me? How would eating alongside them, fighting alongside them, and living with them affect me? Especially if I knew them so well how would their death impact me?

Then after ruining out historical figures to use for the story I thought of mythical ones. Norse mythology figures. Greek mythology figures and so on. However, that's when I finally realized I ran into the same problem constantly. I felt creatively caged. That was because I felt like I had to follow someone else's rules instead of my own. That's why I started looking at superheroes.

Superheroes don't have their own rules that are created from people's own imagination, that's why I created my own.

I'm telling you all this story. Every reader, especially inspiring writers, need to understand that writing a book is not a destination, it's a journey.

The best way I can describe it is by going to a tourist attraction in a country you've never been to. You go to one tourist attraction with an opening to let it take you on a journey of unexpected things you never thought you'd see. You don't go to a tourist attraction where you've already seen everything.

Lastly I want to give a big thank you to my brother for giving me his collection of fantasy books. They helped me a lot while writing a lot. Especially during the final editing stages of the books.

STANDARD V COLLECTOR'S EDITION

If you buy this book in a book store near you will only get the version that has only AFTER DEATH in it and that's it. It is available in eBook, paperback and hardcover.

The collector's edition of the book is only available on Amazon. This version has all the books in one.

This version is called, AFTER DEATH: COLLECTOR'S EDITION.

This version is also available in eBook, paperback and hardcover.

ABOUT THE AUTHOR

Marius Andrei Pintea is a Romanian Canadian author from Alberta Canada. He has 11 published books on Amazon. He is also a filmmaker and journalist, and currently finishing university. Currently in pre-production for a short film called, Curious. While writing his books he also has a YouTube channel called Nina Productions2020. On this YouTube channel he talks about entertainment and giving updates on his books and films.